THE
HAPPY
ADVENTURERS

Lydia Miller Middleton

1st WORLD
LIBRARY
Literary Society

The Happy Adventurers

Lydia Miller Middleton

© 1st World Library – Literary Society, 2004
PO Box 2211
Fairfield, IA 52556
www.1stworldlibrary.org
First Edition

LCCN: 2004195341

Softcover ISBN: 1-4218-0172-8
Hardcover ISBN: 1-4218-0072-1
eBook ISBN: 1-4218-0272-4

Purchase *"The Happy Adventurers"*
as a traditional bound book at:
www.1stWorldLibrary.org/purchase.asp?ISBN=1-4218-0172-8

1st World Library Literary Society is a nonprofit
organization dedicated to promoting literacy by:

- Creating a free internet library accessible from any computer worldwide.
- Hosting writing competitions and offering book publishing scholarships.

The Happy Adventurers
contributed by Tim, Ed & Rodney
in support of
1st World Library Literary Society

CONTENTS

CHAPTER I

How it Began

"Dear, dear!" said Grannie, "woes cluster, as my mother used to say."

"Let us hope that this is the last woe, and that now the luck will turn," said Aunt Mary.

Mollie did not say anything. She had smiled the Guides' smile valiantly through the worst of her misfortunes, but now she was so tired that she felt nothing short of a hammer and two tacks could fasten that smile on to her face any longer. So she closed her eyes and lay back on the cushions, feeling that Fate had done its worst and that no more blows were possible in the immediate future.

Grannie fetched an eiderdown and tucked it cosily round the patient, who looked pale and chilly even on this fine warm day in June, while Aunt Mary tidied away the remains of lotions and bandages left by the doctor.

"The best thing now will be a little sleep," said Grannie, looking down with kind old eyes at her granddaughter, "a little quiet sleep and then a nice tea, with the first strawberries from the garden. I saw quite a number of red ones this morning, and Susan shall give us some cream."

Mollie opened her eyes again and tried to look pleased, but even the thought of strawberries and cream could not make her feel really happy in her heart; for one thing, she still felt rather sick.

"That will be lovely," she said, as gratefully as she could, "and now I think I *will* try to go to sleep, and perhaps forget things for a little while -" and, in spite of all her efforts, a few tears insisted upon rolling down her cheeks as she thought of home, and Mother's disappointment, and the dull time that lay before her.

Mollie Gordon's home was in London, in the somewhat dull district of North Kensington, where her father, Dr. Gordon, had a large but not particularly lucrative practice, and her mother cheerfully made the best of things from Monday morning till Sunday night. There were five children: Mollie and her twin brother Dick; Jean, Billy, and Bob. They lived in a large, ugly house, one of a long row of ugly houses in a dull gardenless street, where the sidewalks were paved, and the plane trees which bordered the road were stunted and dusty. In the near neighbourhood ran a railway line, a car line, and four bus routes, so that noise and dust were familiar elements in the Gordons' lives - so familiar, indeed, that they passed unnoticed.

A month ago Mollie had been in the full swing of mid-term. Every moment of her life had been taken up with lessons, games, and Guiding; the days had been too short for all she wanted to get into them, and, if she had been allowed, she would certainly have followed the poet's advice to "steal a few hours from the night", but, fortunately for herself, she had a sensible mother whose views did not coincide with the poet's.

And then in the midst of all her busyness, just when she thought herself quite indispensable to the school play, the hockey team, and her Patrol, she fell ill with measles. She was not very ill, so far as measles went, but her eyes remained obstinately weak, and so it was decided that she should be sent down to the country to stay with Grannie, do no lessons at all, and spend as much time as possible in the open air. Luckily, or unluckily, according to the point of view, none of the other children had caught the disease, so that Mollie went alone to Chauncery, as Grannie's house in Sussex was called.

Chauncery was an old-fashioned house standing in a beautiful garden surrounded by fields and woods. If Mollie could have had a companion of her own age, she would have been perfectly happy there, in spite of frustrated ambitions and the trial of not being allowed to read; but the very word "measles" frightened away the neighbours, so that no one came to keep her company, and she sometimes felt very lonely. Nevertheless, she had accommodated herself to circumstances, and, between playing golf with Aunt Mary, driving the fat pony, and learning to milk the pretty Guernsey cows, she managed to "put in a very decent time", as she expressed it. Till this third misfortune befell her.

"First measles, then eyes, and now a sprained ankle," she sighed to Aunt Mary on the morning after her accident; "what *can* I do to pass the time? It's all very well for Baden-Powell to talk, but I can't sing and laugh all day for a week; it would drive you crazy if I did. I have smiled till my mouth aches. What shall I do next?"

"You poor chicken!" Aunt Mary exclaimed, with the most comforting sympathy. "You have had a run of bad luck and no mistake! We must invent something. You can't read and you can't sew - how about knitting? Suppose we knit a scarf in school colours for Dick, or a jumper for yourself to wear when you are better? I could get wool in the village. That would do to begin with, till I think of something better."

Mollie agreed that it certainly would be better than doing nothing, though hardly an exciting occupation for an active girl of thirteen. So the scarf was set agoing, whilst Grannie read aloud, and the first half of the first day was got through pretty well. But after lunch the day darkened and rain began to fall in heavy slate-coloured streaks, pouring down the window-panes and streaming across the greenhouse roof, changing the bright daylight into a dismal twilight, and blotting out all view of the garden. It was depressing weather even for people who were quite well, and poor Mollie might be forgiven for finding it hard to keep up her spirits. She was tired of knitting, tired of being read aloud to, and tired of writing letters to her family.

"How would you like to see some photographs of your father when he was little?" suggested Grannie at last. "He was the most beautiful infant I ever saw." She opened a cupboard door as she spoke, and presently came back to Mollie's side with an arm-load of photograph-albums, the kind of albums to be found in country houses, filled with carte-de-visite photographs of old-fashioned people, all standing, apparently, in the same studio, and each resting one hand on the same marble pillar. The ladies wore spreading crinoline skirts, and had hair brushed in smooth bands on either side of their high foreheads; the men wore baggy trousers and beards; family groups were large, and those boys and girls taken separately looked altogether too good for this world.

Mollie smiled at the picture of her father, a fat, solemn baby in his mother's arms. She thought, but did not say, that he was a remarkably plain child, and congratulated herself that she took after her mother in appearance; though, of course, Father, as she knew him, was not in the least like that infant. At the rest of the photographs she looked politely, but it was hard work to keep from yawning, and at last her mouth suddenly opened of itself and gave a great gape.

"That's right," said Grannie, "now I'll tuck you up and lower the blinds, and you'll have a nice little nap till tea-time."

Mollie closed her eyes and tried to sleep, but sleep would not come. She missed her morning walk and the fresh air of out-of-doors, so she gave it up, opened her eyes again, and lay wakefully thinking of home and Mother, Dick and Jean, and school. The big clock on the mantelpiece seemed to go very, very slowly, its tick loud and deliberate, as though it would say: "Don't think you are going to get off one single minute - sixty minutes to the hour you have to live through, and there are still two hours till tea-time." The rain splashed against the window, the wind moaned through the tree-tops, and the room got steadily darker.

"Oh dear!" Mollie whispered to herself, "what *can* I do to make the time pass?"

She sat up and looked round, and her eyes fell upon the last of the photograph-albums - the one she had yawned over. She picked it up, propped it on her knees, and, lying back against the cushions, turned the pages over. These were all children, prim children with tidy hair and solemn faces. Mollie stopped at the picture of a girl dressed in a wide-skirted, sprigged-muslin frock. Her hair fell in plump curls from beneath a broad-brimmed hat with long ribbons floating over one shoulder. Her legs were very conspicuous in white stockings and funny boots with tassels dangling on their fronts.

"I expect this is how Ellen Montgomery looked in *The Wide, Wide World*," Mollie said to herself. "She would be rather pretty if she were properly dressed; she looks about my age. I wonder what sort of time she had - horribly dull, probably. No hockey, no Guiding, no fox-trots - I expect she danced the polka, and recited 'Lives of great men all remind us', and got pi-jawed ten times a day. I can't imagine how children endured life in those days. Thank goodness I wasn't born till 1907! She does look rather nice, though - and oh! I wish you could talk, my dear! I *am* dull."

Just then Aunt Mary began to play the piano in the next room. She played soft, old-fashioned tunes, so that her niece might be soothed to sleep. Mollie did not recognize the tunes but she liked them; they seemed to sympathize with her as she continued to look at the prim little girl in the photograph.

"Perhaps she played those very tunes; she looks as if she practised for one hour a day *regularly*."

As Mollie lay there, the sweet old music sounding in

her ears and her eyes steadily fixed on the face of that other child of long ago, it seemed to her that the child smiled at her.

"I am getting sleepy," she said to herself, and shut her eyes. But she did not feel sleepy and soon opened them again. This time there was no mistake about it - the child in the photograph *was* smiling, first with her solemn eyes, and then with her prim little mouth. Mollie was so startled that she let the album slip from her lap, and it fell down between the sofa and the wall. She turned round, and, after groping in the narrow space for a minute, she succeeded in getting hold of the album again and pulled it up. As she raised her head and sat up, she saw, standing beside her sofa, as large as life, the prim little girl - wide skirts, white stockings, tasselled boots, and all.

As Mollie stared "with all her eyes" as people say, the little girl smiled at her again, and she noticed that, although the child's dress was so very old-fashioned, her smile was quite a To-day smile, so to speak.

"Good gracious!" exclaimed Mollie, "who are you?"

"I am a Time-traveller," the child answered, speaking in a peculiarly soft voice. "You called me, so I came."

"What on earth is a Time-traveller?" asked Mollie, rather surprised to find that she did not feel in the least alarmed at this sudden apparition.

"A person who travels in Time," the child replied. "I am one, and you are one, but everybody isn't one. I can't explain, so you'd better not waste time asking questions if you want to travel. I can't wait here long."

"But -" said Mollie, looking bewildered, as well she might. "Travel where? Of course I'd love to come, but how can I with a crocked-up ankle; and what would Grannie say?"

"Those things don't matter to Time-travellers," said the other child. "We travel about in Time. You haven't got to think about what is happening here and now - that will be all right. But you have to make a vow before you begin Time-travelling. Do you know what a vow is?"

"Of course I do," Mollie replied; "I'm a Girl Guide."

"I don't know what a Girl Guide is," said the other girl, wrinkling up her pretty forehead, "but a Time-traveller has to vow on her faith and honour never to say one single word about her adventures to any grown-up, either here or there. You must not ask them questions that will make them wonder things, however much you want to, because they don't understand, and would be almost sure to interfere. Will you vow?"

"Yes, I will, but you must give me one moment to think. Where shall I travel to and how long shall I stay?"

"You come along with me to my Time; I don't know how long you will stay. A year of our Time might be a minute of yours, or a minute of ours might be a year of yours, but you will be all right. Have you ever seen a dissolving view?"

"That's a magic lantern, isn't it? Yes, Dick once had one. I think they are rather dull."

"Oh no, not if they are properly done. Hugh -" she stopped and then began again. "You will step into a dissolving view of our Time. It just begins and ends anyhow, and you go out of it again."

"But it's so *queer*," Mollie said doubtfully. "I never *heard* of such a thing. I must be dreaming."

The other child shook her head. "No, you're not," she said patiently. She looked around the room as though in search of inspiration, and her eyes fell upon a volume of Shakespeare which Aunt Mary had been reading: "Do you learn Shakespeare at your school?" she asked.

"Rather," Mollie answered, in a slightly superior voice; "I have acted in six plays."

"Ah - then you remember what Hamlet says: 'There are more things in Heaven and earth, Horatio, than are dreamt of in your philosophy'."

"We haven't done *Hamlet* yet," Mollie answered, in a less superior tone, "I don't think I quite understand what that means."

"Neither do I," said the child. "That's it, you see. Papa says -" she stopped short again, and then went on. "It's nearly time for me to go - and I can never come back if you don't come this time," moving away a few steps as she spoke.

"Oh, don't go - don't go," Mollie cried. "I do want to come; it won't do anyone any harm, will it?"

The child smiled very sweetly: "Not the least in the

world. But remember the vow. On your faith and honour."

"I vow, I vow - on my word of honour as a Guide. I can't say more than that."

"Give me your hand, then. Listen to the music, and shut your eyes till I tell you to open them."

Mollie closed her eyes. She had a queer swimmy feeling, as if she were in a high swing and were just swooping down to the lowest point. All the time Aunt Mary's tunes went on, but they seemed to go farther and farther away.

"Open," said a soft voice.

* * * * *

The darkened room had vanished, and the ticking clock; Aunt Mary's tunes and the rain splashing on the window-panes; the sofa too, and the prim child. And Mollie herself!

* * * * *

She was standing in a sunny road, with one foot on a white painted wooden gate, upon which she had evidently been swinging. The gate opened into a large garden, and before her lay a broad path planted on either side with tall, pointed cypress trees, their thin shadows lying across the walk like black bars. Between the trees ran narrow flower-beds, and beyond these stretched a wide, open space, so solidly spread with yellow dandelions that it looked as though the golden floor of heaven had come to rest upon earth.

　　　Lydia Miller Middleton

The path, with its sentinel trees, led straight as a rod to a distant house, long and low, surrounded by a vine-covered veranda. There were strange, sweet smells in the air, which felt soft and warm. The sky was brilliantly blue, and on the fence across the road a gorgeous parrot sat preening its feathers in the sunshine.

Mollie looked about her with curious eyes, wondering where she was. Not in England, of that she was sure - there was a different feel in the air, colours were brighter, scents were stronger, and that radiant parrot would never perch itself so tranquilly upon an English fence.

Then she saw, coming down the path, a girl of about her own age, dressed in a brown-holland overall trimmed with red braid, high to the throat, and belted round the waist. She wore no hat, and her hair fell over her shoulders in plump brown curls. By her side paced a large dog, a rough-haired black-and-white collie with sagacious brown eyes. He leapt forward with a short bark, but the girl laid a restraining hand on his back:

"Down, Laddie, down," she said, "don't you know a friend when you see one? Come in, Mollie."

And suddenly Mollie knew where she was. This was Adelaide, in Australia; that was the child in the photograph, whose name, she knew, was Prudence Campbell; and they were living in the year 1878.

CHAPTER II

The Builders or The Little House

Mollie left the white gate, which swung behind her with a sharp click, and walked up the path towards Prudence. Laddie circled round with a few inquiring sniffs, decided that the newcomer was harmless, and stood blinking his eyes in the sunlight, his bushy tail waving slowly from side to side. Prudence slid an arm through Mollie's.

"I'm so glad you've come," she said. "Hugh's little house is all but finished, and he promised to let us up to-day. Let's go and sit beside Grizzel till he calls."

Mollie's eyes followed the turn of Prue's head, and she saw a younger child seated upon the golden floor beyond the flower-beds. This child wore an overall of bright blue cotton, shaped like Prue's, and her head was covered with short red curls, which shone in the sun like burnished copper. Prudence frowned a little as she looked at her sister:

"How Grizzel can sit in the middle of that yellow, dressed in that blue, with that red hair, I can't think," she said. "She calls herself an artist, but it simply puts my teeth on edge. Did you ever see anything so ugly?"

　Lydia Miller Middleton

"Ugly!" Mollie repeated in surprise. "I think it is beautiful, just like a picture in *Colour*. What is she doing?"

The child looked up at that moment and smiled at them. "Hullo, Mollie," she said in a friendly tone, as if she were quite well acquainted with the new arrival, "come and see my dandelion-chain; it's nearly done."

Prudence jumped the flower-bed, followed by Mollie and the dog, and all three made their way through the thickly growing dandelions, and seated themselves beside Grizzel. She had filled her lap with dandelions, and was busily occupied in linking them together as English children link a daisy-chain.

"What are you doing?" Mollie asked again, as her eyes followed Grizzel's chain, and she observed that it stretched far away out of sight among the trees and bushes.

"I am laying a chain right round the garden," Grizzel replied. "When it is finished it will be the longest dandelion-chain in the world."

"What are you going to do with it?" asked Mollie.

"Nothing," answered Grizzel.

"Then what's the good of making it?" asked Mollie.

"It isn't meant to be any good," answered Grizzel, "it's only meant to be the longest dandelion-chain in the world."

"But there's nothing beautiful about longness ,"

persisted Mollie. "You wouldn't like to have the longest nose in the world."

"It would be rather nice," said Grizzel, working as steadily as the Princess in Hans Andersen's tale of the "White Swans", "then I could smell all the delicious smells there are. Mamma says a primrose-patch in an English wood is delicious."

"Don't waste your breath trying to make Grizzel change her mind," Prudence interposed. "Papa says you might as well explain to a pigling which way you want it to go. Let's help with her chain and get it finished. I'm tired of it." She threw a handful of yellow bloom into Mollie's lap as she spoke, and began herself to link some stalks together in a somewhat dreamy and lazy fashion. Mollie followed her example more briskly.

"It's a pity, you know," she said to Grizzel, "to leave the poor little flowers withering all round the garden when they might have gone on growing for days. They will soon be faded and forgotten."

"I'd rather fade in the longest chain in the world than be one of a million dandelions growing on their roots," Grizzel said, pulling a fresh handful and shifting her chain to make room for them.

Mollie shook her head but did not argue any more. She dropped her chain and looked round the garden. Although the sun was so warm and bright the flowers were those which grow in springtime in England. Daffodils, narcissus, freesias, and violets grew thickly in the borders and under the trees, which seemed to be mostly fruit-trees, though Mollie did not recognize

Lydia Miller Middleton

them all. Peach and apricot were in bloom; fig trees and mulberry trees spread out their broad leaves; and an immense vividly scarlet geranium dazzled even Mollie's modern eyes. It was a funny mixture of seasons, she thought.

Suddenly Prudence jumped to her feet, letting all her dandelions drop unheeded. "There's Hugh!" she exclaimed; "he is calling us. The house must be finished. Come on, Grizzel, leave your old chain - come on, Mollie."

Grizzel shook her head and set all the red curls bobbing; "I must finish my chain first. You go. I won't be long."

Prudence and Mollie jumped the flower-beds again, Laddie, who had fallen comfortably asleep among the dandelions, deciding after a few lazy blinks to stay where he was. A slender boy in grey was waiting for them in the veranda. He was like Prue, but fairer, and his eyes were peculiarly clear and thoughtful.

"Come on," he said, "I'm ready for the furnishings now. What I want is: first, a carpet; second, curtains; and third - third - a tin-opener; but there is no great hurry for that. Where can I get a carpet?"

"Schoolroom hearthrug," Prudence suggested promptly. "No one will notice, and it's pretty shabby since I dropped the red-hot poker and you spilt the treacle-toffee."

"And the curtains?"

" You can have the striped blanket off my bed," said

Prue, after a moment's consideration, "we can cut it in halves."

"Good gracious!" exclaimed Mollie. "Cut a blanket in halves! What will your mother say to that?"

"Mamma won't know," Prudence replied calmly. "She never looks at my bed, and, if she did, she would forget it had ever had a striped blanket on it. Come on, Mollie, we'll get the things and smuggle them across while no one is looking."

Mollie felt shocked for a minute. Doing things behind backs was all against Guide Law, and at home she would almost as soon think of chopping up her own feet as of cutting up Mother's blankets to play with. But, she reflected, different times have different ways; there was no Guide Law in 1878, and perhaps Prue's mother was very extra strict, in which case "all's fair in love and war", so she followed Prue into the house. It was, to her eyes, an unusual sort of house, all built on the ground floor, so that there was no staircase. The front door opened into a square hall with doors on all sides. Prue pushed one open and they passed through into a bedroom, very plainly furnished with two little beds, two chests of drawers, a wash-stand, and a chair. They pulled the white cover off one bed and hauled away a blanket, cheerfully striped in scarlet, purple, yellow, and green, with a few black and white lines thrown in here and there. Mollie thought it would be rather a difficult blanket to forget about. Prue replaced the white cover, spreading it smoothly and neatly, rolled up the blanket, and made for the door again.

Hugh had disappeared. They walked down the veranda, passing several open French windows through which Mollie caught a glimpse of sitting-rooms, and crossed a paved courtyard, at the farther side of which was a red brick house with a wooden porch in front of it.

"The schoolroom is here," Prudence explained, "because Mamma doesn't like noise. It's a very good plan for us; we can do lots of things we couldn't do if we were in the house. Miss Wilton is our governess; she has gone home to-day to nurse a sister with bronchitis. I'm sorry for the sister, but it's a treat for us, especially as Hugh has got a half-holiday. Mamma is out, Bridget has taken Baby for a walk, and Mary is talking to her sweetheart across the fence, so we'll get the hearthrug without any questions."

As she talked, Prudence led the way into the schoolroom. It was plainly furnished and not very tidy, but it had a homely look - in fact it reminded Mollie of the nursery in North Kensington, so that, for one very brief moment, she almost felt homesick. But Prudence gave her little time to indulge in this luxurious sensation (because having a home nice enough to be sick for is a luxury in its way), and Mollie had merely taken in a general impression of books, toys, and shabbiness, when Prudence called her to help with the hearthrug. It certainly was shabby and by no means added to the beauty of the room. They rolled it up with the blanket inside, and, carrying it between them, they left the schoolroom, crossed the courtyard again, scrambled over a low stone wall, and arrived at the foot of a tall tree.

It was a very large tree. Its trunk, grey, smooth, and absolutely straight, rose from the ground for fourteen feet without a branch or foothold of any description. At that height its thick boughs spread out in a broad and even circumference, and across two of these boughs was built a hut, perhaps five by seven feet in area, and high enough for a child of ten to stand upright in. It had a floor, four walls, and a roof, an opening for a door, and three smaller openings for windows. At the door sat Hugh, waiting for the girls and their bundle. When they came to a standstill below him he let down a rope.

"Tie the things on and I'll haul them up," he ordered; "and then you two climb up and give me a hand. Better send Mollie up first, as the ladder is a bit shaky till you know it, and Prue can hang on to it below."

Mollie noticed then that a narrow green ladder leant up against the smooth trunk; it looked as if an unwary step would send it flying, and she put a reluctant foot on the lowest rung. The ground below was hard and stony, most uninviting for a fall.

"You are quite safe so long as you push and don't pull," Prudence assured her. "I am holding on here, and the ladder is firmer than it looks."

Mollie mounted with gingerly tread, but reached the top safely and crawled into the hut through the little door. She was quickly followed by Prudence, and the two girls examined the interior with interest. There was not very much room; two could sit down with comfort, three would be slightly crowded, and four would be a tight fit but not impossible.

"You won't be able to lay the carpet with all of us inside," said Mollie, as she felt the big roll at her back.

"One of you had better stay out," said Hugh. "There are seats all over the tree."

Mollie put her head out at the door and looked up into the branches. They were very much forked, and upon every difficult branch Hugh had nailed steps and made a railing. In some of the forks he had inserted wooden seats, others he had left to nature. The topmost seat was almost at the summit of the tree, and behind it was firmly lashed a flagpole, with a Union Jack hanging limply in the still air, and a lantern with green and red glass on two of its sides. Near the door of the little house there hung from a stout branch a curious-looking canvas bag, broadly tubular in shape, and with a small brass tap at the lower end. The tree was thickly foliaged, but the leaves were delicate and lacy, and, though they formed an admirable screen for the climbers, a good view of the surrounding country was to be obtained between them, and even through them in some places. Mollie decided to climb to the top and look about.

"That's our look-out," Hugh explained. "We can see the enemy from there a long time before the enemy can see us."

"'O Pip', is what *we* call it," said Mollie. "Who is the enemy?"

"It all depends," Hugh replied evasively. "Now, Prue, look alive."

Mollie was a level-headed climber when she had something reasonably solid beneath her feet; no one unfamiliar with the vagaries of the green ladder could be expected to climb it with enthusiasm. She crawled out of the house by the little door again, found her road to the nearest staircase, and climbed this way and that among the leafy branches till she reached the Look-out. There she settled herself comfortably and examined her surroundings near and far, whilst the other two laid the carpet and tacked up the blanket, now cut into three strips by Prudence.

"She looks as if she were hemming sheets for mission-aries," Mollie said to herself, as she watched Prudence doing execution on the blanket with a large pair of scissors. "It would be almost impossible for any girl to be as good as Prue looks; it's her eyelashes, and the way she does her hair."

After admiring the well-planned architecture of the tree Mollie turned her attention to the scenery. At her feet lay the garden with the long, vine-wreathed house and the red schoolroom at one side. It was a large garden, stretching far behind the house, and, as Mollie surveyed the rows of almond trees which outlined its boundaries, she felt some respect for Grizzel's perseve-rance. "If she has laid a chain right round that she knows how to stick to a thing," she thought, as she caught sight of the little blue figure still sitting amongst the golden dandelions. "It's a pity she doesn't do something more worth while. She would make a good Guide." Looking beyond the garden, Mollie could see the town of Adelaide. It was a white town among green trees, with many slender spires and pointed steeples piercing the blue sky, many gardens and meadows, and a silvery streak of river winding across it like a twisted thread. A semicircle of softly swelling hills enclosed the town upon two sides, some of them striped with vineyards, some wooded, and some brilliantly yellow, for the dandelions seemed to be spread over the country like a carpet. Mollie shook a wise head at such waste of good land, for of what use are dandelions! In the far distance she could see a straight white road leading from the town into the hills. She thought she would like to follow that road and see what happened to it in the end. "I had not the least idea," she murmured to herself, "that Adelaide and Australia were like this; not the very least. There must be a great deal of world outside England, when you come to think of it. When I am grown-up -"

"Come down, Mollie," called Prue. "The house is beautiful now; come and see it."

It certainly looked very snug, with the carpet, whose shabbiness was not noticeable in the dim light, and the gaily striped curtains, which had been tacked up and fastened back from the windows. They had added a set of shelves made out of a box covered with American leather and brass-headed nails. A few books lay upon one shelf, and on another stood a collection of cups, saucers, and plates, cracked, perhaps, and not all matching, but suggestive of convivial parties and good cheer. In one corner lay a cushion embroidered in woolwork with magenta roses, pea-green leaves, and orange-coloured daisies, all upon a background of ultramarine blue. Mollie thought it gave an effective touch to the somewhat scanty furnishing - in fact, it was the only furniture there was, except the shelves.

"How perfectly *ripping*!" Mollie exclaimed enthusiastically. "If I had this house I would live in it all the time. It is *much* nicer than a common house in a road. I do think Hugh is the cleverest boy I ever met."

" This is nothing much," Hugh said modestly, "you

should see my raft - that *is* worth seeing. I have invented a way of arranging corks so that it will float in the severest storm. It could not sink if it tried, unless, of course, it became waterlogged. But I can only work at that when we are down at Brighton."

"I wish my brother Dick could be a Time-traveller and come here," sighed Mollie. "He would adore this tree, and the raft too."

"How old is Dick?" Hugh asked with interest.

"He is my twin; we are thirteen and a half," answered Mollie, quite forgetting that in the year 1878 Dick was still minus twenty-nine. "We do everything together in the holidays except football, and just now there isn't any football, so Dick is rather bored at school. In term-time we hardly see each other at all, we are both so horribly busy. How do you find time to do all these things?"

"I don't find it, I steal it," Hugh answered. "If I waited to *find* time I should never have enough to be useful. To-day is a half-holiday, and I am supposed to be learning Roman history and writing out five hundred lines. But I'm not," he added unnecessarily.

"Building is much more important than Roman history," said Mollie decidedly, "and lines are absolutely rotten. I wonder why -"

"Hullo!" came a voice from below. "It's me. I have finished my chain at last, and now I want to come up. Please come and hold the ladder, Prue."

Prudence crept out, tripped lightly down the ladder,

and stood beside her sister.

"Hold tight, Grizzel, and do remember to push and not pull; if you pull I can't hold the ladder up."

"I wish Hugh would cut steps in the tree-trunk like the blacks," Grizzel complained, as she proceeded rather nervously to climb the ladder. "I do hate this old tobbely old green old thing."

"I am going to make a rope-ladder and pull it up after me," Hugh said, watching her from the door of his castle in the air. "I don't want steps that everybody could climb. Look out, Griz, you are pulling -" he stretched out a hand as he spoke, and held the top of the ladder, while Prudence steadied it at the bottom, until Grizzel had safely negotiated "the green passage", as Hugh called it, and crawled in at his little front door.

"It is very, very, very, very nice," she said approvingly, "and it will make a lovely place to come and hate in when everybody is horrid. You can draw the curtains and shut the door, and light your lantern and sit here hating as long as you like, for no one can get up when you have your rope-ladder."

"It would be rather stuffy," Mollie said, looking at the thick blanket curtains. "If he went on hating very long he would be suffocated. I'd sooner have a tea-party myself, and pull all the tea up in baskets. The water would be the hard part."

"The water is in that canvas bag," Hugh pointed out; "Papa gave it to me; it's the boiling that bothers me, because I don't much like using a spirit-lamp in here."

"Get an old biscuit-tin and fasten it up in the tree and put your spirit-lamp in that," suggested Mollie the Guide. "Cut out the front; then you will have a nice little cave all safe and sheltered."

"That's a jolly good idea," said Hugh; "I'll do it to-morrow and we'll have a party."

A bell in the distance warned the children that it was time to go in and tidy up for tea. Grizzel, however, was far too much enthralled by the little house to want to come down so soon. "I don't want any bread-and-butter tea," she announced; "bring me three oranges and eleven biscuits, and the *Swiss Family Robinson*, and let me stay up here."

Tea was laid in the dining-room, where they found Baby already seated in her high chair. She was a very pretty baby, with large dark eyes, silky golden hair, and a dear little mouth parting over two rows of tiny pearly teeth. She gurgled melodiously to her family in the intervals of dropping bits of jammy bread into her mug of milk, and watching them bob about with absorbed interest.

"Good old Mary! She's made potato scones *and* almond gingerbread." Hugh remarked approvingly. "If you've never tasted real Irish potato scones baked on a girdle, Mollie, you'd better chalk it up, as Bridget says. You split them in two, pop in a lump of butter, shut them up, and eat them. Too soon they are but a sweet dream of the past."

"They'll soon be a horrid dream of the future if you gobble them like that," Prudence said warningly, "and you've forgotten Grizzel's oranges; go and pull three fresh ones, and we'd better send her ginger cake."

The gingerbread was baked in thin oblong squares frosted with white sugar, each child's name being written on its own cake in pink letters. They were most fascinating, and Mollie was charmed to see one with her own name on it. The delightful part about this most unexpected visit, she thought, was the way everyone had apparently expected her. She could not help wondering how the invitation had been sent, but decided that it was better not to ask too many questions.

Hugh departed with Grizzel's oranges, biscuits, and gingerbread, elegantly arranged in a green-rush basket, the *Swiss Family Robinson* forming the basis of the repast. He returned with a smile upon his face which disclosed two most engaging dimples.

"I've sneaked the ladder," he said. "Won't Frizzy Grizzy be pleased when she finds out! Ha ha! More scones, please."

"She won't mind," Prudence answered placidly, "she knows someone will have to let her down before Mamma comes in. You've had enough jam, Baby darling; let Prudence take off your bib now and wash your handy-pandys. You can have half my gingerbread if you like, Hugh - hullo, there's Papa!"

There was a sharp double knock at the front door, followed by the sound of someone entering. Prudence set Baby on her feet and bolted helter-skelter across the square hall, flinging herself into the arms of a stout man with a brown beard, who returned her embrace so warmly that Mollie wondered if he had been away from home for some time. He removed his tall silk hat, showing a head as thickly covered with curls as Grizzel's, but the hair was dark and slightly touched with grey.

"Well, my chick-a-biddies," he said, in a delightfully genial voice, beaming upon them all with the kindest blue eyes Mollie had ever seen, "and what has everybody been doing? And where is Grizzel?"

As he spoke he lifted Baby into his arms, ignoring the jammy little fingers, laid a hand on Mollie's head, and looked round inquiringly for his missing daughter.

"She's in my Nest," Hugh replied, "it's finished. Come and see it. You can't climb into it yet, but it looks very nice from the outside. I think I'll arrange a box to pull you and Mamma up in. The zinc-lined box the piano came in would do."

"Thank you, my son," said Papa kindly, "thank you, thank you. At the moment I am rather pressed for time. I have to meet Mamma at Mrs. Taylor's at half-past five, and we are going to the town-hall to hear this wonderful new telephone, as they call it. They say that someone speaking from the post office at Glenelg will be perfectly audible in the town-hall here, a distance of six and a half miles. It sounds almost incredible. What will they discover next! Truly this is an amazing age, and you children may live to see men flying yet."

Hugh had left his gingerbread, which lay forgotten on his plate, and stood before his father flushed with excitement:

" Take me with you, *do*, Papa, " he cried. "I'll learn

reams of Latin and get up at four o'clock and -"

"Well, get your hat and be quick then," Papa interrupted indulgently. "Prue, my pet, look in my bag and you will find five parcels, one for each young robber. Be fair and amiable, my children. Come, Hugh. Good night, Papa's little angel." He kissed Baby, handed her over to Prudence, put on his hat again, and was off down the wide path between the cypress trees with Hugh hanging on his arm, in less than no time.

"Let's watch from the gate," said Prudence. "Bridget will take Baby. Hurry up, Mollie."

They reached the foot of the garden just in time to see Papa's tall hat disappear round the corner of the road. It was a lovely evening, and the girls lingered by the gate; the scent of violets and freesias rose from the flowerbed at their feet, and every now and again came a whiff of something else - something exquisitely fragrant and delicate.

"What's that?" asked Mollie, with an unladylike sniff; "that lovely smell?"

"It's wattle," Prudence answered. "It's in the fields over there. You can smell it for miles sometimes, in the country; it's a nice smell. Let's go and look at Papa's parcels. He went to see Mrs. Macfarline at her toyshop to-day, and when he goes there he always brings something home. It's a beautiful shop. Once I stayed with Lucy Macfarline from Saturday till Monday, and her mamma allowed us to play in the shop on Sunday; it was so funny, all dark and dim, and the dolls looking like little ghosts. We played with the toys on the shelves and had a lovely time. I love shops - oh,

Mollie, we have forgotten Grizzel! She is up in the tree all this time! We must run and get her down. I hope Hugh hasn't hidden the ladder - I wish he wouldn't tease so."

"All brothers do," Mollie said philosophically. "Dick is simply the limit sometimes, but I do wish we could get him over here, Prudence. Do you think we could?"

"I'll think. But first we must find that ladder."

As they neared the tree Prudence called to her sister that they were coming, but got no answer. They jumped the low wall and stood underneath the tree, nearly dislocating their necks in their efforts to see some sign of life in the little house. But Grizzel neither answered nor showed herself, in spite of Prue's eloquent description of Papa's parcels and denunciations of their brother.

"Perhaps she is having her evening hate," suggested Mollie.

"She does take awful fits of the sulks sometimes," Prudence allowed, "but I don't think she would be sulky with *me* just now; it wasn't me that stole the ladder - oh *bother* that Hugh! We had better go and look for it as fast as we can. I wonder where he has hidden it?"

"It can't be far away, because he was only gone for a few minutes at tea-time," Mollie remarked sensibly. "Very likely it is simply lying on the ground behind the wall."

That was precisely where it was, and without much

trouble the girls got it into place again, and Prudence mounted quickly. She disappeared through the little door, but in one moment appeared again with a frightened face.

"She's not here, Mollie. She's gone."

"Gone!" Mollie exclaimed incredulously. "She can't be gone! How could she get down without the ladder? She must be up in the tree."

"No, she isn't. I can see every branch from here; there is not a single place where she could hide."

"But she *must* be up there somewhere," Mollie persisted. "If she had fallen out she would be lying round somewhere. There is no way she *could* get down without the ladder. She is so nervous. I'll come up too and look."

"You may come, but you won't see anything," Prudence said, steadying her end of the ladder while Mollie climbed.

The Nest was certainly empty. The little blue bird must have found wings and flown, Mollie thought. She looked up and down and round about, but not a vestige of Grizzel was there to be seen. Then she called her Scouting lore to her aid, and set her wits to work.

"The basket has gone too, and there is no orange peel anywhere, but the *Swiss Family Robinson* is there on the book-shelf. So she did not go in a great hurry, because she tidied up first. Let us go to the Look-out and see if we can catch sight of her blue frock. She may be hiding quite near and laughing at us all the time."

They climbed to the Look-out and anxiously scanned all the visible parts of the garden, but nowhere was there a morsel of blue pinafore or red curls to be seen.

"We had better get down," Prudence said, "and search the garden properly; I'll ask Bridget to come and help us. What I can't understand is how she got down at all, and, if she *was* down, why she didn't come to meet Papa. She always meets him; always, always. Whoever doesn't meet him Grizzel always does."

Bridget laughed at their fears, but under her laugh Mollie could detect a tone of anxiety, and when house and garden had been searched in vain, Bridget and Prudence faced each other in silence. Then Prue spoke out the fear which Mollie had not understood:

"The blacks have come to town; I saw their wurlies yesterday when we left the Gardens."

"Away wid ye, Miss Prudence," Bridget scoffed. "An' what for wud the blacks be touchin' Grizzel? Isn't yur Pa the kindest gintleman in the whole wurrld to thim, dirrty things they be!"

"Old Sammy was angry because Mamma would not give him a new blanket last time he came," Prudence answered, her face pale with anxiety and tears not far away. "He just goes and sells them, that's what he does, and buys whisky. He followed me all down the road one day when I was alone, and jabbered away till his wife came and hauled him off."

There was a troubled silence while Bridget and Prue

Lydia Miller Middleton

considered the next step to take. Mollie felt that this problem was beyond her powers of solving. Then a sudden thought struck her:

"Where's Laddie? We haven't seen him either."

"Praise be!" exclaimed Bridget. "The dog'll be wid Grizzel, an' that's sure. Blessin's on ye for the thought, Miss Mollie, for it's scared I was an' there's no use denyin'."

"Thank goodness! If the blacks had come Laddie would have barked," Prudence said, taking a long breath of relief. "How on earth did I not miss him myself!"

"Your mind was so full of Grizzel you had no room for another thought, but now - where is she, and how did she get down?"

"We *must* find her before Mamma comes home. Mollie, you are clever; think some more."

Mollie thought her hardest, but, as she explained, it was difficult to make suggestions when she knew neither Grizzel nor the surroundings very well. "She had no hat on; let us go and see if she has taken a hat. Would she be likely to go out without one?"

No, they said, going out without a hat was unheard of. So a search was instituted in the girl's room, and to their relief Grizzel's garden hat was missing - somehow, even to Mollie, it seemed less alarming to be missing with a hat than without one. In fact, if it had not been for the mystery of the tree - which certainly *was* very inexplicable - Mollie would not have

The Happy Adventurers

37

disturbed herself. Grizzel had gone out, wearing her hat, carrying her basket, and accompanied by the large and capable Laddie. Most likely she would come back presently with some simple explanation to account for everything.

"I think she has gone for a walk. She got down somehow and ran off to give Hugh a fright. Let's go and look for her along the road," was Mollie's next proposal.

"If she has gone for a walk she will most likely come home by the lane, unless she went over to the parklands - oh, I wish she would come back! She never goes out alone in town, because she is frightened of meeting Things. She says there are all sorts of Things in town. Once she got lost in a big crowd, and I think it made her rather nervous. Besides, Mamma will be angry if she is not home when they come in, and we'll get such scoldings." Prudence sighed and looked longingly towards the white gate, but there was no sign of the wanderer's return.

"Suppose we go to the Look-out and reconnoitre, and if we see her we can go and meet her," said Mollie.

This seemed a good idea, so they climbed the ladder once more, and, one behind the other, scrambled to the top of the tree. But twilight was already creeping over the land - the brief Australian twilight which turns to darkness so quickly. It was impossible to see any distance, and the girls were turning their backs on the flagpole when Prudence stopped with an exclamation:

"I think I will light the lantern. Grizzel will see it from a long way off. Look in the house for matches, Mollie, while I turn the red glasses both ways."

"But red means danger," Mollie objected, "and we aren't dangerous."

"Mamma is when we break rules," Prudence replied, "and it will remind Grizzel to hurry up."

"Good gracious!" Mollie ejaculated, as she climbed down on her errand, "I am glad we don't hang a red lantern out of the nursery window when we see Mother coming along. How she would laugh if we did!"

"It won't burn long," Prue said, as she shut the lantern door, "but it will do. Now we'll go down the lane; I am almost sure Grizzel will come that way."

They crossed the garden and slipped into the lane through a narrow back gate. It seemed to Mollie that the darkness fell like a curtain, so quickly did it come dropping down. High up above the trees they could see the red lantern shining in the dusk like a glowing ruby; the air was growing chilly, and all the warm bright colours were fading into a dull uniform grey, when suddenly out of the shadowy dimness there leapt a dark form - a form with a bushy tail and a friendly bark.

"Laddie!" exclaimed Prudence, and a moment after Grizzel appeared, running along and swinging her basket.

"Am I late?" she asked breathlessly. "I didn't mean to be so long; I stopped to look at the shop windows."

"Oh, Grizzel, where *have* you been?" Prue said, catching her sister by the arm. "I have been so frightened. Come on quickly now, or we won't be ready, and *then* there will be a hullabuloo and goodness knows what tomorrow."

They hurried back to the house, and were met by an anxious Bridget with Baby in her arms. Bridget scolded, and Baby laughed, and they were all so busy "getting ready" that it was not till three white muslin frocks were spread primly over three green damask Victorian chairs that Prudence found time to ask:

"How on earth did you get down from the tree?"

"I just got down," Grizzel answered, looking mysterious, "I invented a secret way of getting down."

"Nonsense," Prudence said rather crossly; "there can't be a secret way down."

"Well, find out for yourself," Grizzel retorted, her face taking on an obstinate expression.

"But how *did* you?" Mollie asked, with an ingratiating smile.

Grizzel shook her rebellious little red curls. "It's my secret," she repeated; "I won't tell."

"When did you find out that the ladder was gone?" Prue asked, in a more amiable voice.

"I just knew. It's part of the secret."

"You'll have to tell Hugh," Prudence said firmly; "you can't have secret ways into other people's houses."

"I won't tell anyone. It's my mysterious secret and I shall keep it."

Prudence frowned and opened her mouth to speak again, but Mollie signed to her to be silent. Mollie was not a Patrol Leader for nothing; she had learned to be diplomatic, and now she turned the conversation:

"Where are those parcels?" she asked.

"The parcels! Goodness me, I forgot them! How *could* I do such a thing!" Prudence exclaimed, jumping up from the green chair and rushing into the hall, followed by Mollie; Grizzel sat on in sulky dignity, trying to look uninterested.

"Suppose Papa had come home and found we had not opened them, his feelings would have been dreadfully hurt," Prudence said with compunction. "It would have been murder outing. He always says murder will out." Grizzel's dignity could not survive the sight of the brown-paper packages, and the parcels were quickly undone and the wrappings and string tidied away - "the evidences of our folly", Prue said, as she bundled them out of sight. The contents were so charming that everybody forgot their little difference of opinion. There was a fine large kaleidoscope, the first she had ever seen, for Mollie; a charming musical box, with a long list of tunes printed inside the lid and a little gilt key to wind it up with, for Prudence; a Winsor and Newton paint-box for Grizzel; *Five Weeks in a Balloon*, by Jules Verne, for Hugh; and a Punchinello doll on a stick for Baby.

"I must say," Mollie remarked appreciatively, "your father *is* a peach. I have often wanted to see a proper kaleidoscope, but they seem to have gone out of fashion."

The others were too busy admiring their own things to observe Mollie's remarks. Grizzel was speechless with joy as she found all the paints she had been longing for - the crimson lake, Prussian blue, Vandyke brown, and the rest; Prue had wound up her box, and as Mollie turned her kaleidoscope towards the light, and delighted herself with the wonderful colours and designs it produced, she heard the delicate, sweet tinkle of a faintly familiar tune - an old-fashioned sort of tune....

While they were thus pleasantly occupied Professor and Mrs. Campbell and Hugh returned, and Mollie was introduced to "Mamma" who after all did not look in the least alarming. She was a fair, pretty woman, with large clear eyes like Hugh's and a beautifully modulated voice. She kissed Mollie and looked at her with rather a sad expression in her eyes:

"You must tell me all about home this evening," she said in her musical voice. "How nicely your hair is cut; I wonder if Prue's would look nice like that."

"No, no," said Papa, laying his hand on Prue's curls, "I can't spare one hair off my Prue's head. I must have my brown ringlets to play with sometimes."

Hugh could talk of nothing but the wonderful telephone. "I believe I could make one," he said later on. "I understood a good deal of what the man said. I shall require a new magnet and some other things. I'll begin tomorrow." He had forgotten all about such trifles as hidden ladders and treed sisters, and the girls did not remind him.

But when Mollie found herself alone with Grizzel she began to talk about the little house and described a beautiful plan she had concocted for a house-warming, finishing up with the remark that it was a pity that Grizzel could not come.

"Why can't I come?" demanded Grizzel. "Of course I'll come. I adore the little house."

"It's Hugh's house, and I don't think he will let you come if you have a mysterious secret way of getting up and down. He won't like it."

Grizzel was silent. "It's nothing very wonderful," she said at last. "I was only paying Prudence out for forgetting me. She might have remembered to let me down when Papa came home -" and Grizzel's eyes filled with tears. Mollie's heart softened:

"He was in such a hurry that there was no time to get you, and it was my fault afterwards just as much as Prue's."

"I'll tell you now if you like," Grizzel went on; "only you must promise not to tell Prudence and Hugh."

"No," said Mollie, "I can't do that. Prudence was awfully frightened; she got quite pale. We were frightened together and looked for you together; it wouldn't be fair for you to tell me and not to tell her. I hate things that are not fair."

Grizzel was silent again and then sighed. "Oh well, I suppose I'd better tell. I'd have liked to keep one secret, but I can't bear not to go to Hugh's party. It was very easy - I only -"

"Wait," said Mollie, "I'll call Prue."

"I saw Hugh take the ladder," Grizzel went on, after Prue joined them; "of course I heard it scraping along; Hugh is a silly. So I watched him hide it, and when the milkman came I called him, and he put it up and helped me down and we hid it back again. That's all."

The others looked at each other, and then Mollie began to laugh, and went on laughing till Prue and Grizzel laughed at her laughing. "Well, I must say!" she exclaimed at last, "I *am* a Sherlock Holmes and no mistake! I was so busy being clever that I never even thought of a milkman, which would have been Baden-Powell's first idea. Of all the silly things! Why on earth didn't we think of it, Prue?"

Hugh, most reluctantly, went to school next morning, and Mamma kept the girls busy with Italian, music, and needlework till lunch-time. After that Grizzel departed with her paint-box, Bridget took Baby for a walk, and Mollie and Prue settled themselves in the little house, with a cushion apiece at their backs, a basket of freshly pulled oranges between them, and a couple of books in case conversation should flag.

"Now, Prudence, tell me more about Time-travellers," Mollie said; "somehow I can't seem to remember that I am one; in fact -" she paused.

"You can't believe it," Prudence finished for her. "I know. But it's meant to be like that. If you didn't forget you would remember too much, and then you would stop being a Time-traveller, because your mind can't be in two places at once. So it is better *not* to talk; or you may have to go."

"I won't again, but just tell me two things. Can we travel forwards as well as backwards?"

"A few people can, not everyone; but it is better not, Mollie. It is far better not."

"But you came into my Time to fetch me."

"I didn't exactly come, you brought me; and I can only stay a moment."

"Well," Mollie said, after a short silence, "the other thing is: Can I bring Dick? He would love this place and this Time - somehow you seem to have more room than we have, and you are not so frightfully busy. We never have *enough* time; I think your hours must be longer than ours," she went on, with a sigh. "I simply cannot get all the things squeezed in that I want to do. I often wish the days were thirty hours long."

"You weren't wishing that when I came," Prudence said, with a little laugh. "I don't know about Dick; you can't bring him unless he wants to come - of his own accord, I mean."

Mollie pondered a little, and then sighed again: "It will be rather hard. He doesn't want anything frightfully except football, and there isn't any just now. Perhaps we could make him want to come; couldn't Hugh invent some way ? It was only one chance in a hundred - in a thousand, perhaps, that made me talk to your photograph. Let us ask Hugh."

"We can ask," Prudence agreed, "but his head is going to be packed full of telephone now, and he won't think or speak of anything else for days. That's the way he is; we get rather tired of it sometimes, especially when we have to help. Grizzel collected four hundred corks for his raft. She grubbed in the ashpit, and among the empty beer-bottles -" Prudence sighed in her turn.

The two girls met Hugh at the white gate on his return from school, and Mollie seized the first opportunity to make her request.

"I don't know," Hugh answered thoughtfully; "there ought to be a way. I believe there is a way *somewhere* to do everything, if you can only find it. It's mostly a question of looking long enough. And a thing is always in the last place you look for it - naturally. I am going to make a telephone; if I could make one long enough -" he paused.

They were strolling up the wide, cypress-bordered path as they talked, and Mollie's wandering gaze fell upon a low mound at the foot of one of the cypress trees.

"What's that?" she asked, coming to a standstill. "It looks like a cat's grave."

It was a grave sure enough, and crowned with a bunch of pansies. A small headstone had been made from the lid of an old soapbox, on which was printed the following inscription:

> HERE LITH
> THE LONGEST
> DANDY LION CHANE
> IN THE WURLD

"It's Grizzel," said Prudence; "why on earth has she gone and buried her beautiful chain?"

Grizzel joined the group and answered for herself:

"Mollie said the poor flowers would be forgotten. I should hate to be forgotten, so I lifted them all up and buried them. I bought a yard of lovely yellow muslin when I was out yesterday and made a beautiful shroud. That cypress tree is rather big for such a little grave, but it's the littlest in the garden."

No one smiled. "It was a wonderful chain," Mollie said, remembering her view from the Look-out, "I wish I could make something that would reach from here to my brother Dick. I wish we had wireless. I wonder if 'willing' would be any good. Have you ever played willing? We join hands and will with all our might that Dick would come here."

"It sounds easy," said Hugh, always ready for a new experiment, "much easier than making a telephone; we might as well try."

So they joined hands and wished. As they loosened hands again a shrill cry above their heads made them all look up - it was a parrot flying low across the garden, its brilliant plumage shining in the evening sunlight like jewels. " It's my parrot ! " Mollie exclaimed, "it met me by the gate yesterday."

Mollie sat up. The rain was still splashing on the window-panes, but Aunt Mary was drawing the curtains, and a cheerful little fire had been lighted. There was a pleasant tinkle of china as tea-cups were settled on the tray.

"Have I been asleep?" she asked incredulously. (It surely was not all a *dream*!)

"A beautiful sleep," Aunt Mary answered; "and now tea, and after tea - you shall see what you shall see."

CHAPTER III

The Fortune-makers or The Cherry-garden

Mollie was rather silent at tea-time. She could not help thinking of those other children in that long-ago far-away garden. Were they real? Or had it all been a dream? It *must* have been a dream, she thought - such things do not happen in real life - it was impossible that it should have been true. And yet, never before had she dreamt anything so clearly, so "going-on" as she expressed it to herself. She longed to tell Aunt Mary all about it, but the memory of her vow restrained her. If nothing further happened, in course of time she would feel free to tell of her wonderful experience, but in the meantime she must have patience. She racked her brains to think of some roundabout way of introducing the subject of Australia and the year 1878, but could not get past her vow - it seemed to block the way in every direction.

So she ate her little triangles of toast - made in a particularly fascinating way peculiar to Grannie's housekeeping - without enjoying the scrunch, scrunch between her teeth so much as usual. Even the early strawberries and cream found her somewhat absent-minded.

But after tea was cleared away and the room tidied up,

Aunt Mary disappeared for a short time and returned with her hands behind her back. She stood before Mollie, and in a solemn voice chanted the following words:

> "Neevie neevie nick nack,
> Which hand will ye tak?
> Tak the right or tak the wrong,
> I'll beguile ye if I can."

This was too interesting to be ignored. Mollie sat up and became her ordinary self again. She looked critically at Aunt Mary's arms, shoulders, and eyes, but got no information from any of these. Then she laughed:

"I *won't* have the wrong, please, I'll have the right."

Aunt Mary laughed too. "You are too clever, Miss Mollie. That is not the way *I* did neevie-neevie when I was young." She brought her right hand round as she spoke, and in it was a charming box, large, varnished, and clamped at the corners with brass. She laid it on Mollie's lap, and watched the sliding lid being pulled out by a pair of impatient hands. It was a beautiful jig-saw puzzle.

"Oh, where *did* you get it?" Mollie cried joyfully. "I *adore* jig-saw puzzles. You are a lovely, lovely aunt!" and she held out her arms for a hug and a kiss.

"Well," said Aunt Mary, smiling with pleasure at the success of her surprise, "I remembered how fond you are of jig-saws, so yesterday, as soon as you had fallen asleep, I wired to Hamley's. I was not sure if it would arrive to-day, so I did not tell you. Now, let us see what it is - a map! Oh, dear me, I hope you won't find a map dull!"

Grannie, who loved jig-saws almost as much as Mollie did, had drawn up a substantial table to the sofa and seated herself beside it. "Dull!" she said reprovingly, "I hope not indeed. Maps are the most interesting puzzles one can have. What is it a map of?"

"We'll soon find that out," said Mollie, laying a very jagged section upon the table and studying it with interest. "What funny names - Weeah! Where's that? It sounds like China."

Grannie had also possessed herself of a section, and was scrutinizing it through her spectacles. "I'll need my reading-glass, Mary, my dear," she said; "my old eyes cannot see this tiny print."

A silver-handled reading-glass was brought, and Grannie considered her section again: "The Yarra," she read out, "I wonder if you can tell me where the Yarra is, Mollie?"

"Never heard of it," said Mollie, shaking her head. "Yankalilla. Where's that? Goomooroo, Wanrearah, Koolywurtie. *What* names! I am glad I am not a railway guard in this place, wherever it may be."

"Aha, Miss Mollie, I am cleverer than you are with all your Oxford and Cambridge examinations!" Grannie exclaimed triumphantly, "for I can tell you where the Yarra is - it is the river upon which Melbourne is built, and Melbourne is the capital of Victoria, and Victoria is a colony in Australia."

"Australia!" Mollie exclaimed, a little startled. "How funny - I mean how interesting!" It was certainly rather odd, she thought, that her difficulty should be solved so promptly, for now, of course, she might ask as many questions as she pleased and no one would wonder at her sudden interest in our distant colonies. In the meantime Grannie and Aunt Mary were both too much engrossed in the puzzle to notice the rather peculiar expression on Mollie's face, and soon she too became absorbed in the puzzle under her eyes, and forgot for the moment the stranger puzzle in her mind.

When Mollie's breakfast-tray came up next morning, the first thing she saw on it was a letter from Dick. She seized it and tore it open.

"DEAR MOLL,

"I've had the rummest experience you ever. Young Outram says it was-pyh-psy-pysh-ghosts, you know. He says I must tell you *exactly* what happened and not leave out anything, because quite small things might turn out to be most important. Young Outram is great on ghosts and Spirits, he says it is because he was born in the East. It happened like this. Y.O. and me were sitting together at our desk, which is at the back beside the window. It is a very good desk. Old Nosey was talking about *Macbeth* - or perhaps it was *Paradise Lost,* I am not sure of this point, because sometimes he does one and sometimes the other, according to the mood he is in. But it was one of them. Y.O. and I were making a list of Probable Players in next term's 1st XV, and we both said 'Jenkyns will have left', at the same time, so we hooked little fingers and said Kipling, and were wishing a wish when all of a sudden, *without the slightest warning* there appeared, sitting on *our desk,* the most absolutely top-hole parrot I ever saw in my life. We sat staring, because, you see, we never saw the beast fly in, and if it flew through the window we *must* have seen it, because of my arm being on the window-sill. While we were still staring I *distinctly* heard your voice say, 'Do come here, Dick.' Just those words and then no more. Then the parrot vanished absolutely, tail and everything, though it was the finest parrot's tail I ever saw in my life. I can tell you, Moll, it made me sit up hearing you like that. Y.O. said my freckles came out like a rash because I got almost pale under them. I wish I'd seen myself. Then we made the astonishing discovery that none of the other chaps had seen the parrot, in fact they say it is a cock-and-bull story, but we are sitting tight because of the phyc-thingummy. Young O. says that whatever it is he has to be in it too, because most probably it was owing to his peculiar Indian ghostiness that we saw it at all. I don't quite agree, but anyhow that's what he says, and he'd better be in. Please write by return of post if you can explain this phenomenon. We hope you aren't dead.

"Yours affec.,

"DICK."

Mollie read this letter through twice, then laid it down and ate her egg and toast without thinking much of what she was doing. She felt rather startled again; things were certainly queerish. Either her vivid dream had penetrated to Dick's brain - and such experiences were not altogether unknown between the twins - or else - or else Prudence really *had* come yesterday, and there was something in that story of the Time-travellers. So the experiment had worked too. She remembered the brilliant parrot.

She could not make up her mind how much of her story she might tell to Dick. Her vow had only applied to grown-ups, and since the Campbells had helped her to wish Dick over, presumably they would allow her to take him into her confidence. But would he believe such an unlikely story - and what about Young Outram? They had not bargained for two boys. She decided to wait and see if Prudence came again, and, in the meantime, to write and tell Dick that she was alive and well, and that some explanation of his most extraordinary vision would certainly be forthcoming sooner or later.

The morning passed much more quickly than the previous morning had done. Mollie and Grannie worked hard at the jig-saw puzzle, and, without breaking her word by the smallest fraction, Mollie contrived to get a considerable amount of information about Australia from Grannie. Not, of course, that she was totally ignorant on the subject of our Australian colonies, but her knowledge was vague, and her interest before this time had been so faint that it was hardly worth mentioning. Grannie, on the other hand, had had a brother and many friends in Australia, and had, at one time or another, corresponded with a number of people there. She was able to tell Mollie several thrilling tales of bush fires, of the gold-fields, and of Ned Kelly, the great bushranger. But in none of her stories did the name of the Campbells appear.

After lunch Mollie was again tucked up on her sofa and told to take a little nap. Grannie was somewhat amused to be asked for the photograph-album again. "Bairns have queer fancies," she thought to herself, as she laid it on Mollie's lap. "Don't look too long, my lamb," she said aloud. "Try and go to sleep. You were all the better yesterday. There is Aunt Mary playing the piano - dear me, it is long since I heard that tune!"

When Mollie was left alone she opened the album, lay back on her cushions, and stared hard at the picture of prim little Prudence.

"*Now* we shall see! Was it a dream, or will she come again? That is the question."

But nothing happened. Prudence stared solemnly and stolidly back, looking almost too good for human nature's daily food.

"But she wasn't, I feel sure she wasn't, even if it *was* all a dream. Oh - *how* disappointing! I did hope that parrot of Dick's meant something, and I do so want to see those children again and know what happened next. Besides, it would be thrilling to be a Time-traveller - one could see all sorts of things."

As she meditated over her disappointment Mollie turned the pages of the album, looking rather listlessly at the other children, and deciding that none was so attractive as Prudence, till she came to a group of three girls and a boy. She looked closer, then stretched out her hand for the reading-glass and looked again: "I do believe it is - yes, it *is* - Hugh and Prudence and Grizzel and Baby! How I *wish* they would come alive!"

Even as she said the last word she saw a smile dawn upon Prue's face. She did not drop the album this time but held tightly on to it, closed her eyes, and counted twenty. When she opened them there stood Prue, looking as good and sweet as ever.

"Oh, I *am* glad to see you!" Mollie exclaimed, sitting up and holding out her hands. "I thought it was all a dream, and that you were not coming. You will take me with you again, won't you? I did love yesterday."

Prudence smiled and took Mollie's hands in her own. "We need not waste time talking to-day," she said. "Listen to the music."

Mollie shut her eyes and listened to Aunt Mary, who just then began to sing - Mollie could hear the words quite plainly:

> "Oft in the stilly night,
> Ere slumber's chain hath bound me,
> Fond memory brings the light
> Of other days around me."

They were standing on a rough deeply rutted cart-track high up on a hill-side. Behind them the hill rose steeply, so thickly wooded that Mollie could not see plainly to the top. Before her it fell in a gentle slope to a narrow valley, through which ran a shallow creek with green banks on either side. Straight before her, half-way up the opposite hill, she saw a white cottage covered with a scarlet flowering creeper. It had casement windows all wide open, and a trellised porch. The garden of the cottage reached to the foot of the hill, and for three-quarters of its length was filled with rows of vines, looking like green lines ruled on a brown slate.

On one side of the little vineyard Mollie could see a

path winding up the hill, twisting in and out between vines and overhanging trees till it lost itself in a flower-garden, which made such a splash of rosy pink and flaming scarlet that Mollie thought it might have been spilt out of a sunset.

By the roadside at her feet sat Grizzel, red curls still bobbing round her head, and apparently the very same blue overall still clothing her slim little body. She was moulding a lump of wet clay, shaping it into a bowl, pinching here, smoothing there, patting and pressing with both little grubby hands. On a strip of grass before her stood a long row of golden balls, glittering in the sunshine as if they had newly left a jeweller's shop.

Prudence stood beside Mollie, rolling a clay ball round and round in her hands; and Mollie discovered presently that she herself was also rolling a lump of sticky stiff mud into some sort of shape, she was not sure what, but it seemed very important that it should be exactly right.

As she watched the other two children, she saw Grizzel rise to her feet and run a few steps along the road to where, on the upper slope, a wedge had been sliced out of the hill, leaving a three-cornered open space which glittered curiously. This apparently was where the golden balls came from, for Grizzel stooped down, and lifting a handful of shining sand let it filter evenly through her fingers over her bowl. She then set the bowl on the ground, and lightly rubbed the gold sand into its surface. She repeated this process three times, then straightened herself, rubbed her gritty hands on her overall, shook the curls out of her eyes, and said:

" It's quite a nice bowl. If *only* we could make them

hold water, Prue, it would do beautifully for Mamma's Russian violets."

As Grizzel spoke Mollie suddenly realized that she knew where she was. They were in "the hills", across the way was their summer cottage, and those blue-green trees were gum trees. She remembered the long road she had seen from the Look-out, and how she had longed to follow it and see what lay behind those hills.

She carried her ball along to the wedge in the hill-side and rolled it in the golden sand, rubbing it and sprinkling it as she had seen Grizzel do, and soon it took on a splendid yellow shine.

"It looks very nice, Mollie," said Grizzel. "I like the way you've shaped it like an orange. I wonder if I could make a bunch of cherries - I think I will try to-morrow. Put it here beside mine; it is the hottest place."

Mollie stopped and put her ball - which she now saw she *had* shaped like an orange - beside Grizzel's on the sunny patch of grass. Then she stood up and looked round her again.

"Where is Hugh?" she asked, "and Baby, and your father and mother?"

"I think that is Hugh prowling among the roses over the way," Prudence answered, shading her eyes with one hand, and looking across the valley at the garden. "What is he doing, I wonder - he seems to have lost something! Baby is with Bridget. Papa and Mamma haven't come up yet. Miss Hilton is supposed to be taking care of us, but she is rather a goose."

"All the better for us," said Grizzel. "If she were strict and fussy we wouldn't have nearly such a nice time as we do. You have only to say snake to Miss Hilton and she is ready to faint; it is useful sometimes."

"Why should you say snake?" asked Mollie, feeling rather relieved to hear that the elders of the family were away.

"Because there are snakes about, and she is terrified of them," Prudence explained.

"Oh dear - so am I, horribly frightened!" Mollie exclaimed. "I never saw a snake in my life except in the Zoo." "Then how do you know you are frightened of them?" Grizzel asked. "You only have to be a little firm with them and they won't do you any harm. I have lived in Australia for years and years and have never once been bitten."

"I hope I will never meet one when I am alone," Mollie said, shaking an unconvinced head.

While the other children counted their balls, dried their hands, and tied on their sunbonnets, Mollie stood still and gazed about her. The country she saw looked strange and unfamiliar to her eyes. So far as she could see there seemed to be few trees but gum trees, with their monotonous foliage and gaunt grey trunks, so different from the mossy trunks at home in English woods. Here and there one had fallen, and lay like a giant skeleton on the ground. On all sides were hills, not very high, but rolling one behind the other like waves, some wooded and some bare of trees and covered only with short grass and rough boulders. Over everything was the same beautiful clear sunlight that had impressed Mollie so much on her first visit, and the air was warm and soft. She thought of the dull street at home in North Kensington, with brick houses all crowded up together and dingy little back-yards, and she wished that her family could come and live in this wide and sunny country.

As she stood, a cry came across the valley.

"Coo-eee! Cooo-eeeee!"

"There's Bridget calling for tea," said Prudence. "Come on quick; I'm as hungry as a hunter, and Biddy said she would make some damper, because we are rather short of bread."

"What is damper?" asked Mollie, as she followed the other two down the hill. "Is it wet bread?"

"Don't you know what *damper* is?" Grizzel asked, with round eyes. "It is unleavened bread - you know, like the Children of Israel ate. Sometimes we find manna too, lying underneath the trees, but I don't like it much. I am glad I am not a Child of Israel," she added; "I don't like that old Moses. Do you?"

"I haven't thought about him very much," Mollie confessed; "I suppose he was all right in his own way."

"He was so fond of Thou shalt not," Grizzel objected, "and I can't *bear* thou shalt nots. If *I* had made the commandments I should have said 'Thou oughtest not to commit murder, but if thou doest thou shalt be hung'. Don't you think that would be more interesting?"

"No, I don't," Mollie answered decidedly, "I like things to be short and plain like Thou shalt not steal. Then you know where you are."

Prudence looked disapprovingly at her sister. "You should not talk like that, Grizzel; it is flippant, and you know what Papa says about flippancy."

Grizzel made a face but did not answer, and they went on in silence till they reached the foot of the hill. They crossed the little creek by stepping-stones, and walked slowly up the winding path, the vines with their ripening grapes on the one side, and on the other great cherry trees, laden with the largest and reddest cherries that Mollie had ever seen in her life. They hung down temptingly among the green leaves, dangling their little bunches in the most inviting way imaginable, some scarlet, some black, and some almost white, but all ripe and luscious. The children stretched up their hands and pulled some, which tasted as good as they looked.

"I'm going to make cherry jam to-morrow," Grizzel said, dropping her stones on the ground and carefully pushing them into the soil with the heel of her boot. "I'm going to make the first beginnings of my fortune."

"What fortune?" asked Mollie, throwing her stones away in the careless fashion of people who are accustomed to buying their fruit in shops.

"My jam fortune," Grizzel answered. "Every year Mamma sends a case of jam home to Grandmamma, and this year I am going to put in twelve tins of my very own jam, and Grandmamma will sell it and put the money in the bank for me. She promised she would if I was a good girl, and I've been as good as it is possible for a human being to be."

"But can *you* make really-truly jam?" Mollie asked incredulously - Grizzel looked so small and young to be a maker of real jam in shoppy tins.

"Grizzel is a *beautiful* cook," said Prudence, with an air of great pride. "You wait till you taste her herring-shape, and her parsnip sauce. Mamma says that cooks are born, not made, and that Grizzel is born and I'm not made."

Mollie felt an immense respect for Grizzel. Cooking was not her own strong point, as her Guide captain had informed her in plain language more than once, and in any case food at home was too precious for children to experiment with except under supervision - there could be no playing about with fruit and sugar for instance. She began to think that if there were some things she could teach these forty-years-ago children, there were also some things she could learn from them - a thought which would have given her mother much pleasure could she have seen into her daughter's mind at that moment.

"Hullo, girls!" said Hugh, coming out of the garden as they drew near the cottage, "I've got an idea."

Mollie turned to look at Hugh. He had grown a little taller, she thought, but was as clear-eyed and meditative as ever. And behind Hugh was the flower-garden, full of roses - thousands and thousands of roses, mostly pale pink. They were loose-petalled and exquisitely sweet. The children paused for a moment before going into the house, and all four sniffed up the delicate fragrance appreciatively.

"That's my idea," said Hugh, with an extra loud sniff. "Scent! Let's make attar of roses. It costs a guinea a drop to buy, and we could make bottles full. I've been examining the rose-bushes - they are simply packed full of buds behind the flowers. I have been reading about it. It's quite easy to do; you merely have to extract the essential oil from the petals and there you are. I'll show you after tea."

They passed through the porch into the house. There was no hall; they walked straight into the sitting-room, where a table was spread with tea, and Miss Hilton, a rather faded-looking lady of middling age, was already seated behind the tea-pot.

"Go and wash your hands, children," she said, in a voice that matched her looks, "and smooth your hair. I am *surprised* at you coming into the room like this. I don't know what your visitor will think, I am sure. Children have *very* different manners in England."

Mollie glanced round at the other three. She herself stood behind Miss Hilton and was therefore not within that lady's line of vision. She winked largely with her left eye, and a smile of relief travelled round the room.

Tea was a silent meal in spite of the festive damper, which was so good that Mollie thought it must have alleviated the unfortunate lot of the Children of Israel considerably. Hugh was thinking out his plan for making attar of roses; Prue was day-dreaming about nothing in particular, as she was too fond of doing; Grizzel's mind was wandering away to golden bowls, golden cherries, and other possible and some quite impossible golden achievements; while Mollie listened to Baby, who carried on a long and intimate conversation with a family of bread-and-butter - otherwise the beddy-buts - which had found a temporary home upon her plate. Miss Hilton poured out tea absent-mindedly, and seldom spoke except to rebuke someone for putting elbows on the table.

As soon as the meal was over the children went into the garden again, and, once outside, their tongues began to move.

"I shall nab Baby's bronchitis-kettle," Hugh announced, "and make a distiller, and we can begin to-morrow. You girls will have to help me, for I must watch the distilling all the time, and someone must keep me supplied with fresh rose-petals."

"I can't do much, because I'm going to make jam," said Grizzel, "and I want Prue and Mollie to help me to gather cherries. I've got one or two new ideas" - Mollie thought the family seemed great on ideas - "but, if you'll solder up my jam tins, I'll help with your attar."

"I'll tell you what," said Prue, "we'll have a secret breakfast."

"What's a secret breakfast?" asked Mollie.

"You'll see in a minute," Prue answered. "It's a lovely thing. Then we'll get up and pull the cherries and cut them open, and we can pick the roses afterwards, when they are warm and dry."

"Then we had better get the things ready now," said Grizzel.

So while Hugh went off to a little old hut, which

served them for a playroom, to build up his distillery, the three girls set out to inspect the cherry trees, and engaged in the pleasing task of tasting a few cherries off each tree to decide which had the finest flavour.

"I think they are all absolutely topping," said Mollie. "I don't know how you can tell which is best."

"What funny words you use," said Grizzel. "Topping!"

"Well - top-hole then, or ripping, or great, or first-class, or jolly good."

Both hearers laughed. "You had better not let Miss Hilton hear you," said Prue, "or she will tell Mamma, and then you will have to write out 'topping' a hundred times."

Grizzel led the way to the flower-garden, which was laid out on the terrace immediately below the cottage. A sanded path ran along by the rose-bed, which was banked up for two feet or so to keep the soil from washing down in the rainy season. Prudence and Grizzel stopped at a corner where, in a sheltered angle, lay a low pile of bricks built up four-square with a hollow centre.

"This is our fire-place," Prue explained to Mollie. "When we get up very early we make a fire here and boil tea and have a secret breakfast, because proper breakfast isn't till nine o'clock when Miss Hilton is mistress, and we get so hungry - besides, it is a lark."

"Write out 'lark' one hundred times, my dear Prudence," said Grizzel, in a voice so exactly like Miss Hilton's that Mollie looked round with a start, and the other two laughed.

They gathered sticks, which they carried into the kitchen to be dried, Bridget being a good-natured conspirator, and they collected sugar, tea, and damper for their feast. Darkness falls early in Australia, and the children decided to go to bed in good time, so that they should waken fresh in the morning. Mollie thought that their bedroom was a delightful place, quite different from a London bedroom. It had a door to itself, with a flight of wooden steps leading down to the garden, so that the children could slip out without disturbing the household. Mollie thought this very romantic.

"You won't think it very romantic if some old bushranger gets in through the night and shoots you dead," Grizzel cheerfully suggested.

"Be quiet, Grizzel," Prudence said reprovingly. "What is the use of frightening Mollie like that? You never saw a bushranger in your life."

But a London girl, who has been through a dozen air-raids without losing any nerve, is not likely to disturb herself over a possible but improbable bushranger, and indeed Mollie was blissfully ignorant on the subject in spite of Grannie's tales; so she went to bed quite peacefully in the little camp-bed, and lay for a time watching the brilliant stars shine through the wide-open window. The lovely night scents floated in with the soft breeze, and Mollie could hear strange birds calling to their mates at an hour when most English birds are in bed and fast asleep.

The first rosy streaks of dawn saw the three girls making their morning toilet at the pump, where the water was cold even to the touch of English Mollie, but it was freshening, and they emerged from their splashes with pink cheeks and ravenous appetites. The "inventor" loved his bed and did not join in the morning revels. (So boys *were* lazy lie-a-beds in Father's young days, thought Mollie.)

Prudence and Mollie went straight to the cherry trees with their baskets, while Grizzel lighted the fire and prepared the secret breakfast. She called them before the first baskets were quite full. The fire was burning cheerfully, sending long streamers of wood smoke into the morning air. On the bricks sat a billy-can full of water just on the boil, and, as it bubbled up, Grizzel threw in a small handful of tea, giving it a stir round with a cherry twig. She let it bubble again while she counted ten, then lifted the can to one side and put the lid on. She had begged a cup of warm, frothy milk from the milk-boy's pail as he came up the hill. The damper was sitting on the hot bricks, and Grizzel had gathered a plateful of strawberries from the berry-bed at the foot of the hill.

They sat down on the sandy path, holding their mugs of steaming tea in one hand and their damper in the other, large juicy strawberries taking the place of jam. Mollie thought it was the most exquisitely delightful breakfast she had ever tasted in her life. The sun had risen and was sending his beautiful rays along the valley; they fell upon the roses and heliotrope in the garden and on the misty blue-green of the gum trees on the hill opposite. As the children munched in silent enjoyment, their eyes wandering here and there, one long shaft of light fell straight upon the patch of golden sand, so that it glittered as though it were the door to Aladdin's cave. Prue reached out her hand and pulled down a branch of sweet-scented geranium, crushing a leaf and holding it to Mollie's nose.

"Isn't it nice here, Mollie?" she said.

"It's perfectly heavenly," Mollie answered, with a sigh. "Why can't all the world be as nice as this, and why do people *ever* live in streets?"

They tidied up the remains of their breakfast, and were soon back at work in the cherry trees. By nine o'clock they had filled four baskets and had stoned more than half, and laid them in a shallow pan with sugar over them "to draw", as Grizzel explained. They cracked the kernels and took out the tiny white nuts, and last of all Grizzel added a good handful of gooseberries.

"That's my idea," she said, "it will help the cherries to jell. I think I will pop in some red currants too."

"You *are* clever," Mollie said admiringly. "I never in all my life saw a girl as young as you make jam."

"When I am grown up," Grizzel said, sucking her sugary fingers as she spoke, "I am going to have a fruit-farm and make immense quantities of jam to send home. Grandmamma says our jam is the nicest she has tasted, especially our peach and apricot. I am going to try grape jam too, and I shall preserve mandarin oranges whole, and pineapples, and figs."

Mollie suddenly remembered big tins of jam which used to arrive from Australia now and then, at a time when jam was very scarce and precious in London. She smiled to herself as she wondered if they had been Grizzel's jams - they might have been. At any rate they must have come from beautiful gardens like this.

"If you do," she said to Grizzel, "put a picture of yourself and a cherry tree on the tin. It will look much prettier than 'Campbell's Jams'!"

This made the children laugh, and they went in to their second breakfast feeling very cheerful and what Mollie called "pleased with life". The lazy inventor made his appearance halfway through the meal, looking still rather sleepy. "Come and see my distillery," he said, when breakfast was over, "I fixed it up last night."

Hugh had set the bronchitis-kettle - always carried about with Baby, who was subject to croup - on the fire-place, and had fixed a long narrow jam-tin on to the end of the spout.

"I put the roses and water into the kettle," he explained, "and they boil, and the steam comes out and drops into this cold tin and condenses. Then, when we have enough, we boil that up and condense again. Then we skim the oil that rises to the top, and that is attar of roses. It is perfectly simple."

"It *sounds* simple," said Mollie, "but -"

"But what?" asked Hugh, with a frown.

"Oh, I don't know - just but," said Mollie, in a hurry. "I don't know a thing about distilling; how many boilings will it take to collect a bottle of attar?"

"A good many, but you must not forget that a bottle holds a great many drops, and each drop is worth a guinea, so that a lavender-water bottle will hold about three hundred guineas' worth."

Mollie was greatly impressed. How easy it was to make fortunes in Australia! And how much pleasanter a way than Father's way, which meant living in a street and sighing over bills, and not making much of a fortune after all.

The girls returned to the garden, and soon gathered enough petals for the first boiling. Hugh, in the meantime, lit the fire and fetched water from the rain-water tank. "It says water from a spring, in the book," he said, "but there's nothing like rain-water really for this kind of work."

Soon Grizzel said she must go to her jam-making. Prudence stayed to help Hugh, and Mollie decided to hover between both fortune-building schemes, as she was too deeply interested in the results to wish to miss either. For an hour they worked hard, Mollie and Prudence bringing in fresh supplies of roses, rain-water, and logs of wood, for the fire had to be kept well stocked. The room got very hot, for Hugh would not allow any windows to be opened, and a good part of the steam managed to escape in spite of all his care. Indeed it seemed to Mollie that more steam got into the room than into the tin. After the third instalment of roses and water she asked if she could be spared to go and see how the jam was getting on.

"You might bring back some bread and skimmings," said Prudence. "Working like this makes you so hungry."

The day was warm, but it was refreshing to get out of doors after the steamy atmosphere of the playroom.

Mollie sauntered along, keeping in the shade of the trees, a little tired after her early rising. She could see Bridget and Baby at the bottom of the garden gathering gooseberries for a pudding. Baby's pink sun-bonnet bobbed about like a rose going for a walk in the berry-bed. Before she reached the kitchen door she began to smell something uncommonly like burning sugar.

"I expect it has spilt on the stove," she thought; "that pot is pretty heavy for Grizzel to lift."

The smell got stronger and stronger, and when Mollie reached the kitchen there was not only a smell but smoke. There was no sign of Grizzel, nor of anyone else; the house was silent and empty but for the sizzling and smoking of the boiled-over jam. Mollie ran to the stove - a funny flat arrangement, different from the stoves of her acquaintance. The jam had evidently been boiling over for some time, for not only the saucepan, the stove, and the fender, but even the floor was covered with a dark-brown sticky syrup. She trod carefully to the fire-place and lifted the pan to one side, the smoke and steam making her eyes water.

"Making fortunes is pretty hot work in Australia," she muttered to herself. "If I made many there wouldn't be much of me left to enjoy them with. Where on earth is Grizzel?"

She found her in their bedroom, arranging some vine leaves and green grapes in her golden bowl, quite oblivious of a world which contained jam.

"I think your jam is burning, Grizzel - I am afraid it is rather badly burnt."

"My jam!" said Grizzel, coming back to the world of every day. "Goodness me! I forgot all about the jam." She hastily dumped her bowl down on the window-sill, and flew to the kitchen, followed by Mollie.

"Oh dear, dear, dear!" she cried, when her eyes fell upon the scene of devastation. "Oh, my jam! my jam! Oh, why am I *both* a cook and an artist? One half of me is *always* getting into the way of the other half! Oh, Mollie - my lovely, beautiful jam!"

"Let's taste it and see; *perhaps* it isn't burnt," Mollie suggested. But one sip was enough. "Ab-so-lute wash-out!" was her verdict. Grizzel seized the pot by the handle and made for the door.

"What are you going to do?" asked Mollie, following her.

"Bury it," said Grizzel, laying down the pot and seizing a spade. She rapidly dug a shallow hole, poured the sticky black mixture into it and tossed back the earth.

"And they were so pretty a few hours ago," she wailed. "Why on earth did I go and spoil them like that! Oh, Mollie, I am a cruel girl!"

"It isn't *really* any more cruel than eating them," said Mollie consolingly. "I'd just as soon be burnt as eaten myself - only perhaps one might be cooked first and eaten afterwards. I must say it is rather hard lines on mutton when you come to think of it."

Grizzel took the blackened pot to the pump, filled it with water, and carried it back to the kitchen. The fire was nearly out, and logs had to be piled on and blown up with the bellows before the pot could be set on again. Grizzel looked round for a towel to clear up the horrible mess with, but Bridget had washed her towels that morning and they were all hanging out to dry on the line.

"Get a newspaper and crumple it up," suggested Mollie; "wet it in the pot-water."

When Bridget and Baby appeared at the door, two very hot and sticky children were surrounded by a litter of crumpled, wet, black newspapers, and the stove was as far as you can possibly imagine from being clean.

"Holy saints!" said Bridget.

Nothing could have looked less like holy saints than Mollie and Grizzel did at that moment. They stood up in the midst of the ruins, and Mollie waited for the skies to fall. But Biddy was a good-natured soul.

"An' me stove new cleaned this very mornin' - you an' yir jam! Be off wid ye!" flapping the children out of the way with her apron as she spoke.

"Come and wash," said Grizzel, catching up a tin basin from the porch as they went out.

When they were moderately clean again they went back to the playroom to see how the scent-makers were faring. They found Hugh and Prudence as red as lobsters; the big kettle had been moved and a tiny one put in its place.

"I thought I'd better try how the experiment was getting on," Hugh explained to Mollie and Grizzel.

"There's no use doing all the roses till we see if it's all right; so I'm boiling up the distilled water now."

He peered into a doll's milk-jug, which was fastened on to the end of the little spout. "There is a little. We'll just try for oil," he said, lifting the jug off and carrying it to the window. There was about half a teaspoonful of water in the bottom.

"It looks oily; I guess there will be one drop." He sniffed anxiously as he spoke. "And it does smell of roses too, by jiminy!"

They all sniffed in turn, and agreed that there really was an undeniable smell of roses. "And it *might* have only smelt of wet tin," Hugh said. "Look here, Prue, don't empty that little kettle. We'll boil it up again and collect another drop. Put some more logs on the fire."

Prudence looked at Hugh with a slightly exasperated expression; she was very hot and rather tired: "Hugh Campbell, you know as well as I do that there is nothing but tinny water left in that kettle. If you think anyone is going to pay a guinea a drop for scent called Wet Tin you are a goose. I wouldn't buy it if it was the only scent in the world."

Hugh was not discouraged. "My *idea* is right," he said. "I shall make a larger distiller and try again. There's plenty more roses. Next time we are by the sea I shall look for ambergris. It is found floating on the shores of warm countries, and all scent should have ambergris in it, properly speaking."

"I shall try again too," said Grizzel. "There's plenty more cherries, and a new barrel of sugar came

Lydia Miller Middleton

yesterday. After all, everybody has ups and downs when they are making fortunes. I'll take good care never to burn my jam again."

"I'm not really sure if attar of roses is worth while," Hugh said thoughtfully, his eyes on the tiny milk-jug in his hand; "only rich people could afford to buy it. If you want to make a fortune it is better to make something that everyone wants, rich and poor. Soap might do."

"Jam," said Grizzel.

"*I'm* not sure if it is right to make fortunes at all," said Mollie slowly.

"Why not?" asked the other three all at once.

"Because it doesn't seem fair, somehow. Some people are so frightfully rich, and some people haven't even enough to eat. My mother goes to the children's hospital every week, and sometimes she takes me. You can't *think* what some of the poor babies are like - and then you go outside and see rich, *rich* women in splendid motor-cars - I mean carriages," she corrected herself, "and it does make you feel things aren't fair, and I do like fairness."

The Australian children were silent for a minute or two.

"But if no one was rich no one could give," Grizzel said at last. "We know very rich people here, and they do lovely kind things. Mrs. Basil Hill sends us a packing-case of *exquisite* oranges every summer, and when she comes to see Mamma she almost always brings us a surprise packet - last time it was five pounds of the most beautiful sweets in Rundle Street, and the time before it was all Miss Alcott's books."

"But if everybody was the same, people wouldn't have to give you things," said Mollie. "You'd have them yourself."

"Then we would never get a surprise," said Grizzel, "and that would be horribly dull. Don't you think it would be dull if everybody was exactly the same?"

"I suppose it would," Mollie admitted, with a sigh, feeling that she had not presented her case attractively; "but I think they might be samer than they are."

"There's no use talking," Hugh said decisively. "Australia is full of fortunes waiting to be made. I heard Papa say so. And the early bird gets the worm, and the better the bird the better it is for everyone all round."

"Except the worm," said Grizzel.

They all laughed. "I wish I had a brother instead of three sisters," Hugh remarked, emptying the contents of the tiny milk-jug over a handkerchief which had once been clean. "A brother would be some use. Where's yours?" he asked Mollie. "Did he get our message?"

This reminded Mollie of Dick's letter, which impressed the Australians as much as it had impressed Mollie.

"So the next thing - the next thing -" she repeated, looking round at the other three children. "What *is* the next thing to do?"

"We can't tell you," Prudence said, with a funny little smile, "you'll have to fix it yourself in the end."

"Cooo-eeeee!" sounded from the cottage.

* * * * *

"Cherry jam for tea to-day, fresh from the preserving-pan," Aunt Mary was saying. "That will be a treat for you, Mollie, my dear."

CHAPTER IV

The Treasure-hunters or The Duke's Nose

"Cherry jam is certainly very *runny*," said Aunt Mary at tea-time.

"Do you put a handful of gooseberries into it?" Mollie asked rather dreamily, as she tried in vain to spread her scone tidily.

"Gooseberries! Why, no; I never thought of it. It might be quite a good idea."

"Or red currants?" Mollie went on.

"Red currants! Bless the child! I didn't know you were a cook, Mollie."

"Neither I am," said Mollie, rousing herself up to the fact that she was back in Chauncery, and must set a watch upon her tongue. Why was it, she wondered, that she forgot Chauncery so much more when she was with those other children than she forgot the children when she was at Chauncery? "I once heard a person say they put gooseberries and red currants into cherry jam, and I suddenly remembered," she told Aunt Mary.

" Well, it is too late for cherries, but I will try it for the

Lydia Miller Middleton

strawberries to-morrow. It will be quite an interesting experiment."

Mollie resolutely pushed her thoughts about the cherry garden and its occupants into the background, and gave her whole mind to a game of patience with Grannie, who was getting a little tired of jig-saw. But when that was over, and Grannie was absorbed in casting on a stocking-top with an intricate pattern, while Aunt Mary wrote letters, she began again to think and wonder about her curious journey, which for some reason seemed less strange to-day than it had done yesterday. She pondered over ways and means to get Dick across, or over, or through, "or whatever you call it when you travel in Time", she thought; "back might be the best word. I do *wish* I could tell Aunt Mary."

She looked thoughtfully at her aunt, whose head was bent over her writing, the smooth bands of her silky, brown hair shining brightly in the lamp-light. No doubt some, perhaps most, grown-ups would scoff at her tale if she told it, Mollie thought. Grown-up people as a rule love best to jog along on well-trodden, safe, commonplace paths, and avoid adventurous by-ways, but Aunt Mary, Mollie felt sure, was an anti-jogger, so to speak, and would always choose adventures if she had a choice. "It's funny to think," Mollie reflected, "that she can't be so very much younger than Mrs. Campbell is - was - is - was then. I suppose she is about thirty-five, and Mrs. Campbell forty or so - she looks - looked old enough to be Aunt Mary's mother. Being good at games keeps her young; she can beat me to a frazzle at golf and tennis; and she is frightfully keen on aeroplanes; I'm sure she would fly if it weren't for Grannie. I wonder why she never got married?"

Mollie had not yet come to the age of sentiment, but now and then she reached forward a little and surveyed its possibilities, and now she paused awhile to muse upon the subject of her aunt's spinsterhood. Not for long, however; she decided that Aunt Mary must have had excellent reasons of her own for remaining single, and returned to the more pressing problem of how to get Dick into the Campbells' garden. Finally she thought of a plan worth trying.

"Grannie, may I have the loan of one of your photographs?" she asked. "Dick has a way of copying them with a thing he has that makes them look like drawings, and the old-fashioned ones are the prettiest."

"By all means, if he will be careful," Grannie answered, nine-tenths of her mind being fixed on her new pattern and only one-tenth upon her grandchild's peculiar fancy for Victorian photographs. So Mollie wrote a short letter to her brother, enclosing the group which had worked the magic charm for herself that afternoon. She put it into the evening post-bag with a sigh. "If that doesn't do it I *can't* think of anything else," she said to herself.

It is remarkable how quickly one becomes used to a new routine. Already Mollie was making more use of her hands and head because she could not use her feet. She was fond of writing, and decided next morning to begin an account of her strange adventure while it was still fresh in her mind. In the intervals of other plans for her future career she had dreams of becoming a writer of books, but her difficulty hitherto had been that the usual sort of book is so ordinary, and she had never been able to think of anything remarkably unusual to write about. The autobiography of a person who could live in various periods of the Christian Era might turn out to be quite interesting, she thought, if only people would believe that it was true. The trouble was that most likely they would think she was inventing it, "and anyone can *invent* any old thing. And this is only the beginning of my adventures. When I have thoroughly learnt how to Time-travel I will go back much further - perhaps to the French Revolution, and watch people being guillotined."

She scribbled diligently in the thick exercise-book, which Aunt Mary produced without once asking what it was wanted for. "It just shows - " Mollie murmured gratefully; "some people would have teased me to death."

And so time passed, and half-past two came round again in the usual inevitable way, and Mollie lay expecting Prudence as calmly as though she were coming from next door. She had the album on her lap, and was turning the pages in search of a new photograph, when in the twinkling of an eye Prue was there.

"We don't need that now," she said, "but we must have Aunt Mary's tunes. Where is she?"

"Oh dear, dear, I forgot!" Mollie cried in dismay. "I do believe Aunt Mary is making strawberry jam, and I went and told her about putting in gooseberries and red currants, and her head will be full of them and she will forget me!"

But the lullaby had not been forgotten. At that very moment the piano began - a tune Mollie knew well this time, for she had often heard the American soldiers sing it in London:

"Oh, darkies, how my heart grows weary,
Far from the old folks at home".

"Give me your hand - quick," said Prue in a whisper.

*   *   *   *   *

Mollie found herself standing on a wide beach in the curve of a beautiful bay. Before her lay the sea, dark blue in the distance, a clear emerald green by the shore. To the right of her the beach stretched as far as she could see, firm yellow sand on the lower half, fine white silvery sand higher up. On the left it only ran for a couple of miles or so and then ended in rocks, over which the sea threw a cool white spray. Behind her, Mollie saw, when she turned, the line of the beach was followed by sandhills, some covered with low-growing scrub and some quite bare and treeless, shining like snow in the hot sunlight.

The children were all there. At a little distance from where she stood Mollie could see Hugh and Prudence, Hugh lightly clad in a swimming-suit, and Prue with her skirts rolled up and her feet bare. A wide sun-hat covered her head, and her brown curls were fastened back with a clasp, which made her look older, Mollie thought.

The two children were hauling a large, square, flat object down to the sea, Hugh pulling in front with ropes, and Prudence pushing behind.

"I do believe it's the raft," thought Mollie. "This must be Brighton, and I suppose the summer holidays have come round again. It is a little difficult to keep up with Time here. I do *wish* Dick could come!"

Grizzel was sitting on the beach close beside her, and seemed to be gathering shells from a little pale-rose patch on the sand at her feet. She was very absorbed in her task, but she looked up at Mollie with a smile, apparently not at all surprised to see her there. She was dressed, like Prue, in a turned-up overall and wore a wide hat, which hid the red curls from view and gave her an unfamiliar look. Bridget was sitting not far from Grizzel, busily doing crochet-work and singing a song about a wild Irish boy, while her eyes wandered after Baby, who was singing a little song of her own invention about a poor lonely whale who had a loving heart. Higher up the beach, at the foot of the sandhills, Mollie could see Professor and Mrs. Campbell, one reading aloud and the other sewing.

"Where shall I go first?" Mollie asked herself, "I think I'll go and see what Hugh and Prudence are doing."

She found, when she began to walk, that she was bare-legged and bunchy about the skirts like the other girls, and that her head was covered with a sun-hat like theirs, a tanned Panama straw, light as a feather, and shading her eyes from the glare of sea and sand. The sun was very hot and the sand was warm under her feet.

"Hullo! Here's Mollie the Jolly!" exclaimed Hugh, as she drew near. "Come along and lend a hand - we are just about to launch the good ship *Nancy Lee* on her trial trip."

Mollie examined the raft with deep interest. It was

really very neatly made, the planks straight and smooth, and firmly held together by cross-bars underneath. There was a mast in the exact centre, with a sail at present close-reefed, and there was a pair of old oars which, Hugh explained, had been purchased from a boatman of his acquaintance. All round the raft were bunches of corks, several hundreds at least.

"Did Prue and Grizzel find all those?" Mollie asked.

"We all collected 'em," Hugh replied; "lots of people gave us corks - jolly old winebibbers they must be," he added ungratefully. "Now then - with a long, long pull and a strong, strong pull!"

They got to the edge of the water, and the two girls waded in as far as they could go without getting their clothes wet, before the raft finally took to her natural element and rocked up and down on the smoothly rippling wavelets. A gentle breeze was blowing off the sea, but the tide was running out, which, Hugh remarked, was a good plan, as the raft would go out to sea with the tide and come back with the wind in her sail. He thought, however, that he would not carry any passengers on the first trip - in fact, to begin with, he would harness himself to his craft and pull her both out and in, "just till I see how she goes; she's got to find her sea-legs."

The girls watched the raft and its owner depart into deep water; they saw Hugh climb on board, and decided that the passengers who sailed aboard the *Nancy Lee* would be most suitably attired in bathing-dresses, as she appeared to slide along as much below the ocean as above it. After standing for some minutes they wandered along towards Grizzel, who was still

Lydia Miller Middleton

sitting by the pale rosy patch on the sand. When they sat down beside her Mollie saw that the shells she was gathering were so tiny that they were hardly larger than a pin's head, and yet they were perfect in form and colour; she thought she had never seen anything more exquisite.

"We thread them and make necklaces," Prudence explained; "they are so thin that you can stick a needle through them quite easily; they come in beds like this all along the beach. There are lots of lovely shells here, and sea-eggs too. We collect them sometimes, but our collections have such a way of getting lost somehow, they are always beginning over again and ending too soon."

"Can you say 'She sells sea-shells' twenty times running, as fast as lightning?" asked Grizzel.

"Not running as fast as lightning," Mollie answered, "but I could say it if I were walking rather slowly."

"I couldn't," said Grizzel, taking no notice of Mollie's flippancy, "if I were to crawl at the rate of half an inch a year I should be saying 'She shells sea-shells' the whole time."

"You are talking nonsense," said Prudence. "Come up and see Papa and Mamma."

Mollie was greeted kindly by the older people. She had forgotten to ask if she was supposed to be a visitor or only spending the day with the Campbells, but gathered from Mamma's conversation that she was paying a visit and had arrived that morning. She wondered again how they heard about her coming; the children appeared to take her for granted, but, of course, *they* knew she was a Time-traveller!

As the girls sat by their elders, idly playing with the silvery sand and chatting to each other, a large steamship came in view, coming from the north and heading south-west. They all stopped working and talking as they watched her steaming along, a trail of smoke blowing behind her, smudging the blue sky with clouds, black at first and gradually fading to grey.

"That's the English mail," Papa said at last; "she was due to leave the Semaphore at three o'clock to-day."

They were silent again; the great ship drew nearer - now she was almost opposite.

"Oh - John - *Home!*" Mamma said. There was a tremble in her voice that made Prudence and Mollie look up - there were tears in her eyes.

"I know, little wife, I know," Papa answered softly, putting a hand over the white hands which had dropped the busy needle.

The girls rose to their feet and left Papa and Mamma. They went down to the edge of the shore, and stood watching the ship as she began to slip over the horizon.

"Now she has begun to go down the Big Hill," said Prue. "She will sail for miles and miles and thousands of miles, and for days and nights and weeks across all that sea. I wonder if some children on the other side will be playing on that beach, and will watch her funnel climb over the top of the hill again and say: 'Here comes the Australian mail!'"

Mollie did not answer. She could not remember ever taking much interest in the Australian mail. But in future she determined she would always watch when she had the chance, and wave a friendly hand to the incoming ships.

Soon there was nothing to be seen of the big steamer but a trail of smoke, which lingered long in the sky.

Prudence had fallen into a day-dream; and Mollie's eyes were roaming over the blue sea, when suddenly she caught sight of the raft bobbing about on the little waves, sometimes above and sometimes below. In the water in front of the raft she could see Hugh's head, like a round black ball - and - yes, she was not mistaken, there were two other round black balls which must also be heads. That was rather odd, she thought; she had not noticed any other boys about.

"Look, Prue!" she exclaimed, catching Prue by the arm, "look - there is Hugh, and he has got someone with him - oh, *do* you think he has rescued some drowning sailors?"

Prue came out of her day-dream with a jerk, and brought her thoughts and her eyes back to earth, or rather to sea.

"Yes, he *has* someone with him," she said. "How funny!"

As they gazed, the three swimmers turned round and, with a good deal of ducking and slipping, climbed aboard the raft, which triumphantly survived and remained afloat, though decidedly wet about the deck. They proceeded to unfurl the sail, which one boy held while the other two took to the oars, and, after some hard work, the *Nancy Lee* was safely beached. Grizzel joined Mollie and Prudence, and the three girls watched the three boys, not offering to go and help with the raft because they felt a little shy of the strangers.

Presently one of them turned round - and Mollie gave a jump. The boy's hair hung over his forehead in wet, black streaks, and he was dressed, or rather undressed, in a swimming-suit, the rest of him being wet, white skin; but in spite of this unusual appearance Mollie was almost sure - in fact she was quite sure - that it was Young Outram. And the other boy - who kept his back turned in a provoking way as he examined the raft - why, *that* boy - yes, it surely was Dick! Mollie squealed and caught Prue by the arm:

"It's Dick and Jerry Outram!" she exclaimed, jumping up and down with excitement. "Oh, Prue - have they swum all the way from London without any clothes?"

Prudence laughed. "Mollie, you *are* a goose! *Do* you think they could swim fourteen thousand miles?"

"Well how -? Oh, I forgot! It is so hard to remember about Time-travelling here! Oh, Prue, *how* exciting it is!"

At that moment Dick looked round and saw his sister. Both boys came racing along the sand towards the girls, kicking up their heels like young colts.

"Cheerio!" cried Dick, as he pranced up. "What price school! How's this for a rag? Jolly old beano, I call it!"

"What does he say?" asked Grizzel.

"He says that school isn't much of a place, and that this is a great lark, and that he enjoys being here immensely," translated Mollie. "*Some* psychical phenomena!" exclaimed Young Outram, prancing up in his turn.

"I'm afraid we haven't got any," said Prudence politely.

"And you forgot to say 'Please' if we had," said Grizzel, with a frown.

"*What* do they say?" asked Young Outram, looking puzzled.

"Prudence thought you were asking for some what's-its-name-how-much," Mollie explained again.

"What *does* he mean then?" Grizzel asked.

"He means that this is the loveliest magic that he ever heard of," said Mollie. "You shouldn't use such long words, Jerry, and they aren't true either, for this is *not* thingummy phenomena, it is simply common everyday magic."

"There is no such thing as common magic," said Jerry.

"There is," said Mollie.

"There isn't," said Jerry.

"What do you call it when your mother gives you a dirty little brown onion to put in the ground and you bring it back to her turned into a parrot-tulip?"

asked Mollie.

"Oh - if you -"

"Stow it, Young Outram, you blighter," Dick interrupted. "Don't be such a silly old Juggins, making them ratty first go-off like that. Keep your hair on, Mollie, and don't get the hump over nothing. If you *must* jaw about parrots, jaw about the dossy chap we spotted in school; you are simply talking hot air, both of you."

"*What* does he say?" asked Hugh, who had come up by this time.

"I wish to goodness you boys would speak plain English," Mollie said impatiently. "I don't want to spend all my time explaining you to the others."

"Irry yourry tawrry lierry tharry weerry wirry tawrry lierry thirry, arry therry yourry woerry urrystarry wurry wurry tharry weerry sayrry," said Grizzel, rather angrily and very rapidly.

"*What* does she say?" asked both boys at once.

"It's only our private language," said Prudence; "she says that if you talk that way we'll talk our way, and then you won't understand us. *That* wouldn't do any good. I think we'd better have a Circle. Give me your hand, Mollie, and you take Hugh's. And Hugh Dick's, and Dick Grizzel's, and Grizzel Young Outram's, and Young Outram my other hand. Now all stand quite still and shut your eyes; listen to the waves, and try and think of three nice things about the people next you."

The six children stood in a circle, silent and still, as Prudence had ordered, their eyes tightly closed. They felt the hot beams of the sun pouring over them, and the cool salt wind blew on their faces and through their hair; their toes curled and wriggled in the warm, wet sand, and in their ears was the plash-plash of the little waves beating backwards and forwards on the beach. It was very pleasant. It seemed quite easy to think of those three nice things. And presently each child felt a warm and friendly glow steal up its left arm, through its heart, down its right arm - and so on to its neighbour. When this pleasing and cheerful sensation had gone round the Circle three times, Prudence said: "Now, open your eyes and let go."

They stood there smiling at each other, and feeling almost ready to burst with goodness and loving kindness towards all the world.

"Now we'll understand each other," said Prue. "Words don't matter much if you understand people. Now what shall we do?"

"Don't let's stand about any more," said Mollie; "the time does go so quickly, and there are lovely things to do. What would you like to do, Young Outram?"

"Call me Jerry all the time," he answered first. "I want to forget about school while I can - there are a good many of us at school," he explained to Prudence, "and we are called Old Outram, and Outram Two, and Young Outram; and there are three Outram Kids at the prep, and another kid at home."

"*All* boys!" exclaimed Prudence.

Jerry nodded. There had been nine Outram boys before the war! "Let's go out on the raft again - please," he added, with a wink at Grizzel, who smiled back. "You come too; we could easily push you along."

"We'll have to change into our bathing things first," said Prudence; "the raft looks a little wet. We won't be long."

The girls ran up into the sandhills to change, but before Prue disappeared she returned to the boys with a basket made of rushes in her hand, which she had begged from Bridget.

"Here are some buns and grapes," she said a little shyly, "I thought you might be feeling hungry, and it is a long time yet till tea-time."

Jerry decided on the spot that if he ever *did* go in for the peculiar entertainment of falling in love, he would choose a shy girl with brown curls who did not talk slang and went about distributing buns to hungry boys. "Her for mine," he expressed it to himself.

The girls were soon back, all in navy-blue bathing-suits, knickers below, and a belted tunic reaching to their knees above - too much clothed for Mollie's taste; she liked to be skimpy when she went swimming. But no one grumbles after they have been in a Circle - at least, not for the next twenty-four hours - so Mollie endured her substantial garments philosophically and soon forgot all about them.

The girls waded out to the raft, which the boys had launched. They climbed on board and were soon in fairly deep water. Mollie and Prudence slipped off and left lazy Grizzel alone on deck, sitting cross-legged like a little tailor, one arm flung round the mast. The raft rocked gently up and down on the calm sea, while the children swam, ducked, and played about in the clear, sun-warmed water like a school of young porpoises. As Grizzel sat idly watching the rest, her eyes fell upon an object which floated at a little distance from the raft. It was a bottle - a common beer-bottle - its cork rammed well in and sealed with red wax.

"What's that?" she called to Hugh, pointing to the bottle as it danced about, twirling round and round, tossing from side to side in the wide ripples sent out by the children and the drifting raft.

They all made for it. "It's a message from the deep," cried Jerry; "probably from a ship-wrecked sailor."

Hugh, being the nearest, caught it by its red neck, and the whole party collected on and about the raft to see what would happen next. But Hugh refused to break the bottle until they went ashore again.

"The sea might get in and spoil the paper, and the broken glass would get on deck and cut us; we'll pull her in now and read the message on the beach," he decided.

They got under way and, practice making perfect, were soon high and dry on the beach, and the *Nancy Lee* dragged up and comfortably moored. The children seated themselves in a ring, and Hugh cautiously knocked off the neck of the bottle with a stone. He drew out a paper, which had been carefully rolled round a thin bamboo stick and tied with a red ribbon.

There was no date on the paper, nor was there any sign to show where the bottle had been thrown in, but written in large, clear round-hand was the following message:

IF THE FINDER OF THIS BOTTLE
WILL SEARCH THE CAVE UNDER
THE DUKE'S NOSE HE WILL FIND
SOMETHING TO HIS ADVANTAGE.

"Hidden treasure," said three boys all at once. "Where is The Duke's Nose?" asked Dick.

"Never heard of it," answered Hugh, looking hard at Jerry, whose nose was distinctly aquiline and promised to be more so in the future. "You aren't a duke by any chance, I suppose?" he asked.

"No, old sport, I'm not," Jerry answered, with a grin, "and if I were, the only treasure you would find in the cave under my nose would be some jolly sharp teeth, and they wouldn't be at all to your advantage either."

"It's probably among those rocks over there," Mollie suggested; "I expect if we went there and walked round we would see something that looked like a duke's nose."

"But there aren't any big enough to have a cave under them," said Prudence; "they are all quite little rocks."

"It will be a bit of the cliff, most likely," said Dick, "in fact it is almost bound to be if there is a cave."

The others agreed that this was probable. "What do you think the hidden treasure will be?" asked Grizzel.

"A sack of diamonds and rubies?"

"I hope not," said Jerry, "for, if it is anything of that sort, we will have to give it up. If we were caught trying to sell diamonds we'd be copped at once, and the bobbies would think the bottle story was all made up. I expect we'd all be put in jail, and it would be jolly awkward for Dick and me when we got back to school. I think I see the Old Man's face when we explained that we couldn't come because we were in an Australian prison in the year 1879 for stealing diamonds. I don't think!"

"Schoolmasters and mistresses are extraordinarily stupid sometimes," said Mollie reflectively. "They are so hard to convince, even about quite simple things, if they don't want to be convinced. But I shouldn't care for diamonds myself. I'd like a swanky tennis-racket."

"I'd like a revolver, latest pattern," said Jerry.

"I should like a first-class camera," said Hugh.

"I'd like a pure-bred bull-dog," said Dick.

"I'd like a nice little model sewing-machine," said Prue.

"I'd like six pairs of stilts," said Grizzel, "and then we could all walk home on them."

Everyone looked a little ashamed; Grizzel was the only one who had thought of the five others. A murmur went round that of course they had *meant* six of everything. Then Mollie began to laugh: "How funny we will look if we each get all the things," she giggled.

"We will walk home on the stilts, with a revolver and a sewing-machine tied on to each stilt, and a tennis-racket and a camera on our backs, and six bull-dogs trotting after us."

This flight of fancy made everyone laugh consumedly: "We must go home now, anyway," Prudence said, as she dried a tear, "because it is getting on for tea-time and we have got to get dressed. Perhaps there will be time to go to the rocks after tea and just *look* for a nose, and if we find it we'll take some spades in the morning and dig."

The Campbell's seaside cottage stood behind the sandhills. It had been built by a retired sea-captain, who had planned it to look as like a ship inside as a house could be made to look. The walls were panelled in wood, painted bird's-egg blue, and decorated with pictures of ships. The windows were round like portholes; the table stood across one end of the room and was screwed to the floor, as were also the benches on either side. In the children's rooms were bunks, in rows one above the other, and the washing-stands were fixtures. It was altogether very charming and romantic.

Tea was of the kind called high, and the hungry children disposed of cold ham, an extraordinary number of boiled eggs, several loaves of smoking hot new bread, and at least a pound of butter and two or three pounds of jam.

"May we go for a walk to the rocks?" asked Prudence, when tea was over. "We will go very quietly along the beach and not get wet, and be home before dark."

Papa said he would walk that way a little later on and

meet them; so Mamma gave permission, and soon a party of six were wandering by the shore towards the rocks, carrying their boots and stockings slung round their necks. It did not take them long to cover the two miles which lay between their beach and the rocks. Mollie found it hard to pass by all the lovely shells with which the beach was strewn, but the rest were impatient. The sun was dropping down the sky and they had not too much time for their search.

It did not promise to be a very successful search, for nowhere was there anything even remotely like a duke's nose to be seen - nor indeed any sort of nose. The rocks were low and for the most part jagged, with pools of water in the hollows between them for unwary or careless people to slip into. Many of them were covered with periwinkles, which Grizzel could not resist gathering. She filled her boots with them.

"Papa likes them," she said, when Prudence and Mollie remonstrated with her for lingering; "he says they taste like a sea-breeze, and if we aren't going to take back a duke's nose I may as well take a periwinkle's nose; it will be better than nothing."

The cliffs were high and precipitous, but they were no particular shape, being, as Hugh said, merely the edge of Australia. The children scrambled along till they reached the turn of the coast-line, beyond which were more rocks and cliffs, much the same as those about them.

"Perhaps it isn't here at all," Prudence said, as they seated themselves in a row on the edge of a big boulder; "the message didn't say it was. It might be anywhere. Perhaps that bottle came hundreds of miles, and the Duke's Nose is at the South Pole."

"More likely Kangaroo Island or Yorke's Peninsula," Hugh said. "We might sail the raft across - it's only about fifty miles to the Peninsula."

"How'd you get her to go?" asked Jerry. "We couldn't swim fifty miles; half a mile is my limit at a stretch; Dick can do three-quarters."

"We'd have to use the sail and tack a bit, and we'd have the oars."

"What about food?" asked Prudence.

"We'd sling it in a can on the mast. Water's the trouble; we'd have to distil sea-water, and that takes coal and might be a bit difficult; there isn't a place for coal on board yet."

Mollie remembered the attar of roses and decided not to embark upon that voyage. "We would be pretty thirsty before there was enough water distilled for us all to drink," she thought to herself.

"Well, we'll have to be getting home now," said Prudence, with a sigh. "It will be dark before so very long."

A somewhat silent and subdued party set out on the homeward scramble, the boys in front, Mollie and Prue together, and Grizzel in the rear, being hampered by her bootfuls of periwinkles, which would keep falling out. She stopped at last, and, sitting down, she laced her boots tightly up and tied the tops round with the lace ends. When she looked up from this task she

Lydia Miller Middleton

stopped again to admire the gorgeous sunset. The whole sky was ablaze, and the sea had changed from blue to crimson and gold; the wet beach was gleaming like an opal, pale-rose and lavender, with fiery amber lights shimmering on the rippled sand. The brilliant glow of the western sky was reflected in the east, and the cliffs stood out sharply against the light, themselves flushed with pink. Grizzel's keen young gaze ran along the outline, black where it cut the sky.

"There's nothing there," she said to herself, "only that flagstaff hut, and it's as square as square."

As she watched, a door opened in the side of the hut and a man came out, swinging a billy-can in his hand. Suddenly Grizzel caught her breath. Where had she heard someone say that that hut was a tiny refreshment-bar, where a man could go in and get boiling water for his tea - that everlasting tea which the Australian drinks at any and every hour of the day? It was Papa, and he had said they called the hut 'The Nose' - short, Grizzel felt sure, for The Duke's Nose. Her eyes ran quickly down the cliff underneath - yes, she could see the cave quite plainly when she looked hard, though to the casual glance it looked like a deep crevice in the cliff.

She looked after the others. They had scrambled on ahead while she was tying up her periwinkles, and were now too far away to hear anything but a shout. She put her two hands up to her mouth and gave the long shrill "Cooo-eeeee!" of the Australian-born child, which caused five heads to be turned in her direction instantaneously. Prudence started running back, fearing that her sister had fallen and hurt herself. Grizzel's gesticulations made things no plainer to the others - when she pointed to the hut they thought she meant them to get help, so that Hugh and Dick set off towards the cliff, while Jerry came on with Mollie and Prudence in case there should be a broken limb.

Even when they got within hailing distance they did not understand, for what between keeping a foothold on the slippery rocks, hanging on to her periwinkles, and her excitement over her discovery, Grizzel was getting breathless and incoherent, and all she did was to point a small forefinger at the hut and say: "Duke's-nose-you-know-duke's-nose-you-know-your - nose-dukes-know."

"She is delirious with pain," said Mollie, "and she is mixing the Duke's Nose up with 'She sells sea-shells'."

However, it was not very long before they reached her side, and she was able to explain the situation. A few more excited coo-ees brought the boys back, and the question became: What to do next? The sun was getting perilously near the horizon, and once it dropped behind the sea, darkness would fall rapidly and the rocks be really unsafe, especially as the tide was now coming in.

"We must get up frightfully early in the morning," said Dick at last, "and come along before breakfast. Nobody is likely to find that treasure in the next ten hours or so."

With many backward looks they resumed their homeward trek. It was hard luck to have to leave the treasure when, perhaps, they had almost found it, but Mamma's word was law, and if they broke their promise about getting home, or at least meeting Papa, it was quite possible that to-morrow would be spent by the girls in doing French verbs and making buttonholes.

The children slept soundly all night in their funny little bunks. Early in the morning a small figure slipped into the boys' room and shook first one boy and then another by the shoulders. Dick and Jerry woke up after a few grunts; Hugh as usual was a sleepy-head.

"Leave him to us," Dick said confidently, "*we'll* get him up - you'll see."

"Tell him to come by Gobbler's Hollow," ordered Grizzel; "you'll find us there. Don't stop to wash."

When the boys were half-way across the sandhills, they saw a thin column of blue smoke rising from somewhere among the low scrubby trees, and a minute after a delicious smell greeted their unducal noses - a smell of wood-smoke and toast combined.

"It's the girls making grub," Hugh explained to the other two; "they're great on grub." He might have added that he was great on it himself, so far as eating it was concerned. Certainly Dick and Jerry were very pleased to know that they had not to wait until half-past eight for breakfast, for the fresh sea air had given them ravenous appetites. They found the girls in Gobbler's Hollow - appropriately so named by Hugh - bending over a gipsy fire. The inevitable billy-can hung from a tripod, and the steam from it mingled with the smoke of the fire. Mollie was toasting bread, which Prudence buttered with a lavish hand, and Grizzel was shelling hard-boiled eggs.

"I call this top-hole," Dick announced, as he squatted

down on the sand and took his tin mug from Mollie, who had begged to be allowed to make the tea as she had seen Grizzel make it before. "It will buck us up no end and make us as sharp as needles."

They were in a hurry to get on; so when breakfast was done they pushed the mugs and knives into the hollow of a bush, which Grizzel explained was their store-room. Later in the day the girls would come back and tidy up; for the present the great thing was to get to the cave as quickly as possible. They had two clear hours before them in which to make their search.

The tide was at its lowest, and there was a broad stretch of wet sand between the sandhills and the sea. Wide shallow pools of water had been left behind by the receding waves, while here and there lay long heavy drifts of seaweed, shining darkly in the early rays of the morning sunlight. The children splashed their way along, their eyes fixed on the flagstaff hut. As they drew nearer they left the sea and steered for the cave, the entrance to which was plain enough now that they knew where to look for it.

"It's such a conspicuous sort of cave," Hugh said, "I don't see how anyone could miss finding treasure unless it is buried very deep."

Caves have always a certain amount of mystery about them, but this one was undoubtedly as ordinary looking a cave as one could find. It did not burrow very far back into the cliff side, and what there was of it was open to the daylight and contained no lurking dark corners. The walls were rough and rocky but not high; the roof was, as Jerry said, nothing particular, and the floor was of shingle and rather wet, as if the sea, now so far away, had paid it a visit not so very long ago. But, as the rocks and stones before the entrance were dry, it was obviously not the tide which had washed the floor.

"It must be a spring or something," Hugh said; "let's taste and see - " he stooped as he spoke and scooped up a handful of water, which he put to his lips.

"Thought so; it's quite fresh and sweet - that's rather a find - jolly useful for picnics, it will save us carting water about - by jinks!" he exclaimed, looking round at the others with an expression of blank dismay; "do you suppose *that's* what we were to find to our advantage?"

They all stared hard at the shining wet stones, through which the trickle of water was now plainly discernable. Then they stared round the cave again. There did not seem to be a place where treasure *could* be hidden. Moreover, there were traces of a not very remote picnic - the dead ashes of a gipsy fire, one or two crumpled-up balls of paper, some broken bottles!

"That's it," said Jerry at last. "It was probably the people who had that picnic - those broken bottles are the same as the one we found. They played cock-shy with them, and then thought it would be a lark to chuck one into the sea. What a jolly old sell!"

"We've had a nice morning anyhow," said Prudence, "and the spring certainly *will* be an advantage when we've got used to it not being a sewing-machine and bull-dogs and things."

"I somehow don't believe it is the spring," said Mollie thoughtfully, still staring about her. "There is something about the way that paper is written; it doesn't look like the writing of the sort of person who plays that kind of joke - and of course it would be meant for a joke. Let's all stand quite still in a circle back to back, and each stare hard all over the bit of cave that comes in front of us, and see if there isn't a sign of some sort."

They agreed that there would be no harm in trying this plan, though the boys' hopes were small. Dick and Jerry were uneasily conscious that they were "the sort of person" who would have thought that bottled message an excellent joke - to play on someone else!

So they stared. They even circled slowly round so that each part of the cave was examined with meticulous care by six pairs of eyes in turn. But it was all in vain; the cave only seemed to become more and more ordinary the longer they looked at it.

"There's not a place where you could hide a thimble," Prue said sadly, "let alone a treasure."

"What's that?" Grizzel called out suddenly, pointing to the broken bottles in the corner.

After all there *had* been a dark spot, and with the brightening daylight that dark spot had all at once lighted up, and there lay a bottle, the very twin of the one they had found in the sea, red sealing-wax and all. The boys made a dive for it, but Dick stopped abruptly and held back the others: "Grizzel saw it first, let her open it too," he said.

Grizzel advanced, and picking up the bottle held it to the light - yes, there was a message plainly to be seen.

"I think one of you had better break it open," she said; "I'd probably cut my fingers."

Hugh solemnly knocked off its head and drew out the paper. It was written in the same round, clear handwriting:

IF THE PERSON WHO FINDS THIS
BOTTLE WILL ASK FOR MR. BROWN
AT THE DUKE'S NOSE, HE WILL
HEAR OF SOMETHING TO HIS ADVANTAGE.

"Why the dickens couldn't they have said that first shot?" Jerry exclaimed.

"I expect Mr. Brown will tell us to go to the Duchess's Toes and hear of something to our *dis*-advantage," said Hugh sarcastically.

"If we are going to look for Mr. Brown we will have to hurry," said Prudence, who had gone to the entrance of the cave and was scrutinizing the beach; "by the look of the shadows I should say it was a good bit after seven. In not much more than an hour we must be sitting down at breakfast tidy and brushed."

They found when they came out that there was a footpath up to the Duke's Nose - a very steep and boulder-strewn path, but quite a possible one for them all; so they went for it manfully and womanfully and were soon at top. But alas! the door of the hut was closed and locked; no one answered their repeated knocks, and they came to the unwilling conclusion that the place was empty.

" Blow ! " said Dick at last. "Why couldn't the old

treasure-hider put his old treasure in an easier place?"

"If he had, someone else would have found it," Mollie remarked sensibly, "and anyhow it is a lark searching for it."

At that moment a man's figure could be seen coming towards the hut; he was swinging a billy-can by the handle.

"That's the man I saw last night," exclaimed Grizzel; "I expect he is Mr. Brown."

The man was rather surprised to see six children congregated before his hut door at that hour of the morning. Prudence was pushed forward as spokeswoman. "Please, are you Mr. Brown?" she asked, in her most polite voice.

"I am, miss. Anything I can do for you?"

"We found this piece of paper," she said, showing the latest message to him, "and we brought it to you like it says."

The man grinned broadly - he had a nice grin, the children thought - "You've found it, have you? Well, that beats me! That's darned clever of you. Our little Missie will be no end bucked to hear that bit o' news; she was mighty taken up with her messages, she was. You'll have to wait a bit, though. I can't leave this place before twelve noon. You be on the beach above where that big hump o' seaweed is at twelve-thirty today, an' you'll see -" the man broke off and grinned again.

"What?" asked several excited people at once.

"That's tellin'," said Mr. Brown; "just you wait an' you'll see somethin' to your advantage, same as it says here."

It was terribly hard to have to leave the treasure at this thrilling stage, but there was nothing else to be done, especially as it was getting late, and they would have to hasten their steps as it was, if they were to reach home in time for a proper tidy-up before breakfast. Mamma was very particular about many things, but she was particularly particular about coming to table with clean hands and freshly brushed hair.

*   *   *   *   *

They were at the trysting-place long before half-past twelve. Nobody had a watch, but the Australian children had a device of their own for telling the time.

"You stand on one foot," Hugh explained, "and twirl round with your other big toe in the sand - like this. That makes a circle to fit your own shadow. Then you stand in the middle and see where the shadow hits the circle. And then you guess the time near enough for all practical purposes. It's quite simple."

"Did you invent that sort of clock yourself?" Mollie asked deferentially.

"There wasn't much to invent," Hugh replied modestly; "it's on the same principle as a sundial. I only applied my legs."

"God invented Hugh's legs and the sun," Grizzel said;

"Hugh only put in the squiggly toe."

"But that's just it," Jerry argued; "like Newton and the apple. The simple things are there all the time, and no one sees them till the right person comes along. I think that's a jolly ingenious idea. You'd have to know exactly where due north was, of course, and you'd have to have the sun. That's the trouble in London; the sun just slops about the sky, and half the time you can't see him at all."

The children now twirled round and round like dervishes, making shadow-clocks till there were hardly any shadows left, as the sun rose higher and higher in the heavens. It also became warmer and warmer; so they decided to sit in a row with their backs to the sea and their eyes firmly fixed upon the hut, determined not to miss the sight of the treasure for a single moment.

"Let's play 'I went to market with a green umbrella'," Prue suggested, "and we can think of all the things the treasure might be." The green umbrella had been to market about twenty times when a voice behind them made them all start.

"Well, now - to be sure!"

And there was Mr. Brown, with nothing in his hands - no sack upon his back.

"How *did* you come, Mr. Brown?" Mollie asked. "We looked and looked."

"Grand sentries you'd make - all lookin' one way," said Mr. Brown."Suppose you look at the sea for a change."

Six pairs of eyes turned to gaze at the sea - and six pairs of feet instantly began to run, for there, drawn up on the beach, was a boat!

"How's that for a tidy craft?" asked Mr. Brown. "Is she pretty shaped? How do you like her paint? Look at her nice little oars. Eight, she holds - nice-sized party eight is, sort o' cosy an' cheerful."

The children looked from the boat to Mr. Brown and back again. Nobody thought any more of stilts or sewing-machines, or even of bull-dogs; the only thing on earth worth having at that moment was the wonderful boat around which they were standing. Her outer dress was of bright, dark green, with a scarlet line round the rim; inside she was pure white. A little railing of delicate iron scroll-work ran round her stern, and across it curved a board, with the boat's name in scarlet and gold: *The Belle of Canada.*

"Do you mean -" Hugh began, but he was too over-powered to finish, because it was all very well to talk about cameras and things in the abstract, but that such a thing as a real, life-sized boat - and such a beautiful boat too - should fall into their hands in this casual way was too wildly improbable to be true.

But it was true, nevertheless. That lovely little boat was really theirs!

The way it happened was this, Mr. Brown explained: the year before - while the Campbells were in the hills - a little Canadian girl, visiting her Australian relations, had come with them to stay in the very cottage the Campbells were in now. She was very ill when she arrived. The doctors feared consumption, and said that open air all day long was the best medicine she could have. So the boat was bought - "and a fine price they paid for her too," Mr. Brown remarked - and the little girl was half her time on the sea, and got so sun-burnt and sturdy that before she left she was rowing the boat herself - "an' you'd never know she'd had a mite the matter with her," Mr. Brown said. When the time came for her to leave she took a fancy to give her boat to some other children, so that they might have as happy a summer with it as she had had. But it wasn't enough to give it in the usual way of giving - she made up the plan of the message in the bottle, which she left with Mr. Brown.

"But I wasn't in no hurry," he said. "I kep' my eye on the cottage children. The last lot were a rampagin' set o' young ruffians, smashin' everything they set hands on. I soon saw that this chap was a different sort altogether, hammerin' an' tinkerin' away at his raft, and careful of her as if she was a lady - he's the sort for little Missie an' me, I said to myself, so in the bottle went, only an hour or two before you found it."

"And suppose no one had found it, or the other bottle?" Dick suggested.

"Not much danger o' that, with six pair o' sharp eyes an' inquisitive headpieces around," Mr. Brown answered, with a laugh. "The only bit I wasn't sure about was the Duke's Nose, for not many knows it by that name; but little Missie would have it - said it was more romantic like, though what's romantic about a duke's nose it beats me to see - just like any other nose, I don't mind bettin'."

"Hugh says Jerry's nose is like a duke's," Grizzel said,

so that all eyes were immediately fixed upon poor Jerry's nose.

"Jolly romantic, especially when I have a cold in the head!" he exclaimed.

"Well now, jump in, the lot o' you, an' I'll row you along to your Pa," said Mr. Brown.

"Do you know Papa?" asked Grizzel, whose round blue eyes had never left Mr. Brown's face since he began his story.

"Yes, I know your Pa. There ain't many round here that don't. Now then -"

As Mr. Brown talked he had pushed the boat out, with some help from the boys, and had lifted the girls in. Now he took the oars, and, with a few powerful strokes, he sent the boat skimming over the sparkling blue sea.

All the children could row, more or less, but Mr. Brown gave them some useful hints. "An' you mustn't ever go far out to sea by yourselves," he said, "nor yet too near the rocks except it be a calm day like to-day. Remember that a good sailor won't ever run his ship into danger unless he can't help himself, no more than he would his wife. If you want to go a regular excursion to the Port or such, you can always get one of us to go with you, unless, of course, your Pa can take you. But you'll get plenty of fun, an' learn a lot too, playin' round here - you'll learn the feel o' the sea, which is something quite different from rowin' on a river. An' don't you be givin' the raft the go-by," he added, addressing himself to Hugh; "there's a lot goes to a raft an' you never know when your knowledge o' handlin' one may come in useful. That's a tidy one you've made, but it wants a bit o' tar. I'll bring some along one o' these days an' show you how to use it - there's your Pa wavin' to you."

An excited party of children landed on the beach and told their story to Papa, whose consent had to be won before the lovely boat was really theirs. He was as delighted as they were themselves, and an expedition was planned for that very evening, to include Mamma and her guitar.

"If you will give me the little girl's address I will write and tell her all about how we found the bottle," Prudence said to Mr. Brown, "and we will all write and say 'Thank you' for her *beautiful* idea."

"She's back in Canada now," Mr. Brown answered. "She'd be mighty pleased to hear from you."

It was difficult to sit down soberly to boiled mutton and batter pudding after these exhilarating adventures, but it had to be done, and after dinner the girls had to "sit quietly with their needles" for an hour; but at last tea-time came, and evening followed, and the whole family except Baby embarked upon the first voyage in *The Belle of Canada*. It was delightful to float about on the moonlit water and listen to Mamma's lovely voice. She sang a Canadian boat-song, in honour of the little hostess in far-away Canada:

"From the lone sheiling of the misty island
Mountains divide us, and the waste of seas -
Yet still the blood is strong, the heart is Highland,
And we in dreams behold the Hebrides.

"Fair these broad meads - these hoary woods are grand; But we are exiles from our father's land."

Silence fell upon them all after that. Mamma's white hands dropped from the guitar and slipped under Papa's arm; Prudence thought in her dreamy way of the little Canadian; Mollie remembered the American soldiers and their song; Hugh's mind was full to the brim of boats and rafts and ships.

"Look here!" cried Jerry suddenly; "we're a good slice of our jolly old Empire to-night - Great Britain, Australia, India, sailing in a Canadian boat - there's another song we ought to sing - " he jumped to his feet as he spoke, making the boat rock in the silvery water. "Come on!" he sang:

"Rule, Britannia! Britannia rule the waves!"

*   *   *   *   *

"Oh, Jerry! *Why* did you go and do that?" Mollie called out, as she sat up and rubbed her eyes. "It isn't nearly time to wake up yet!"

"Indeed it is, you little lazy bones," Aunt Mary said, with a laugh. "Goodness, child! You are beginning to look quite rosy and sunburnt! Spraining your ankle seems to suit you. I think I'll sprain mine and see if I can raise a complexion like that. It's as good as a visit to the seaside."

"Ah!" said Mollie.

CHAPTER V

The Gold-diggers or The Miracle

"DEAR MOLL,

"This is exactly what happened yesterday. Young Outram says that it is very important for us to keep notes, in case the Thingummy Society should want to know all about it one of these days.

"To begin with I was late for breakfast, so I grabbed your letter and stuck it in my pocket, along with a roll, and bolted. Everything as usual till about 2.30. Bibs was trying to knock some maths into our heads, which I call pretty hard luck on a chap who has crawled to the top of his left wing while shots were dropping round like hail. He looked fairly fed-up. It was tremendously hot and my head ached, and Young Outram had a rag-nail on his first finger which he said was causing him frightful agony, when I suddenly remembered the roll and found your letter. So we ate the roll and read it, I mean we read your letter and ate it - anyway, we were looking at that photograph and thinking that the boy looked a pretty decent sort, and wishing we were him instead of ourselves when suddenly he appeared! He really did, I'm not making this up. At the window just where the parrot was yesterday. And the funny thing is that we don't usually sit at that desk for maths, but the

Lydia Miller Middleton

other room was having something done to it, so we did yesterday. The chap stared at us, and Y. O. said, 'Hullo!' and he said, 'Hullo!' And Y. O. said, 'Who are you?' And he said, 'I'm a Time-traveller!' And we said, 'What the dickens is a Time-traveller?' And he said 'Like to come and see?' And we said, 'You bet your hat!' And he said, 'Hold my fist and shut your eyes!' So we did, and next thing we knew we were floating on our backs in the sea as calm and cool as cucumbers, and the raft was bobbing about, and you know the rest. At least, we suppose you do. That's what we want to know. Hugh told us the Time-traveller yarn. It sounds a fairly tall tale, but we've heard taller from chaps who were at the front. The point is, how can we go back? London is a rotten hole in this weather.

"Your affec. bro.,

"DICK."

Mollie read this letter as she ate her morning oatcake. So her spell had worked! The question was, would it work again? For obviously she could not continue sending away photographs without causing remarks to be made and questions asked. She did not see how she could do anything more herself; they must just trust to luck, at any rate till she saw Prudence again.

It was rather odd, when she came to think of it, that she had not questioned Dick yesterday about how they had got over. But the fact was that, after the first surprise of seeing them, she had forgotten. "I forget about Now and only remember Then," she said to herself. "There is so much to do the time simply flies and comes to an end far too soon."

When she arrived downstairs that morning she found that her sofa had been carried out of doors. It was a lovely day. Here in the country the leaves still retained their early freshness, and from where she lay she could see the downs, mistily green against the pale morning blue of the sky. The rose-garden, with its smoothly mown grass paths, its pergolas and arches, its standards and dwarfs, was coming into bloom so fast under the June sunshine that Mollie thought she might almost see a bud swell into a full-blown rose if she watched steadily enough. Caroline Testout had already dropped some of her pink blossoms, which lay scattered about the path in rosy patches, reminding Mollie of Grizzel and her shells. She smiled to herself and then sighed, as her eyes wandered from the rose-garden to the long red brick wall beyond, where the sweet cherries grew. The fruit was turning scarlet under an orderly net, which had been put up to protect it from the greedy little birds. Everything was so tidy, she thought. No one would dare to pull off those rose petals for scent-making purposes, nor to gather those cherries merely to play at making jam with. Chauncery was lovely and spacious compared to the house in North Kensington, and the well-kept gardens were a pleasure to look at, but -

"I don't think England is big enough to hold children," she said to Aunt Mary, who sat near, reading the *Aeroplane*, with some neglected needlework lying in her lap.

Aunt Mary looked up with a surprised expression: "I am sorry you are feeling so crowded up," she said. "Would you like me to move a little farther away?"

"No, thank you," Mollie answered, with a laugh, "I

Lydia Miller Middleton

have room to breathe even with you there. What I mean is -" she paused for a moment, wrinkling her brow, and then went on: "London isn't like this; it's full of poky holes. Ours is bad enough, but from the train you can see much, much worse places than ours. Sometimes I wonder how people can live in them, and yet Mother says they are not the worst. There is simply no room for children to play, so they play on the streets and sometimes get killed. The Girl Guides are going to help, but it takes a long time " - Mollie shook her head thoughtfully - "and there is so little time too; at home I never have any time to do anything except work or Guiding. I have no time to think in, except after I am in bed, and I go to sleep so horribly soon." She shook her head again and sighed deeply.

"Well, that's one good thing to be thankful for," Aunt Mary said cheerfully, dropping her paper and taking up her sewing, "and there are the holidays for thinking in. I wouldn't think too much, if I were you. You'll get plenty of that when you are old," and Aunt Mary sighed too, as if she did not find her own thoughts very gay affairs always.

"But I want to think of things now that will be useful long before I am old," Mollie persisted. "There is such a *tremendous* lot of things to be done, Aunt Mary. And things have to be thoughts long before they are things. I expect the person who invented aeroplanes thought about them for ages and ages before he began to make one."

"I haven't the slightest doubt of it," Aunt Mary agreed, "but you are wandering from your subject, which was the smallness of Great Britain."

"No, I'm not - at least not exactly, I want to make Great Britain greater, and I can't think of a way. I should like to have plenty of room and plenty of time."

"That won't be an easy problem for you to solve, my lambkin," Aunt Mary said. "As a matter of fact there is room enough, in the country, but people prefer to live in towns. You will have to hire a pied piper and pipe all the babies into the fields."

Mollie shook her head, her eyes resting again upon the distant downs. "I don't know," she said seriously, "but something will have to be done some day, Aunt Mary, besides play-centres. They are good, but they aren't enough. Too many children die. Mother goes to a children's home once a week, and she took me once. You should just see those babies. And they could be such dear little things too. Why - " Mollie hesitated for a moment and then went on, "Why don't more people go to live in Australia and Canada? The maps are full of empty spaces."

"Ah, Mollie my dear, that's not so easy as it sounds," Aunt Mary said, folding up her work and rising to her feet. "There are all sorts of complications when it comes to shifting camp from the Old World to the New. But perhaps - perhaps if everyone in this old country could be persuaded to think of the children first - ! In the meantime I must go and get lunch for my particular child."

Probably Aunt Mary's mind was running on those sick babies of the poor as she played to Mollie that afternoon, for her fingers wandered off into the tune of a song she had not heard sung since her childhood:

"'T is the song, the sigh of the weary:
Hard times, hard times, come again no more!
Many days you have lingered around our cottage
door
Oh, hard times, come again no more!"

Mollie lay listening, the unopened album in her lap. She was drowsy after her morning in the garden, and thought she would rest her eyes by closing them for five minutes. "A little darkness will do them good after all that sunshine," she murmured to herself.

It was very pleasant lying in the quiet room, on that broad sofa, listening to Aunt Mary's soft music. Mingling with the sound of the piano was the droning hum of a foolish bee, who had got on the wrong side of the window and was now making vain efforts to fly home again through the glass. A delicious scent came from somewhere - perhaps from the syringa bushes growing just outside the open window. Mollie's lazy eyelids fell over her eyes - "Just five minutes -"

"Five minutes," said the clock. "Ten minutes. Fifteen minutes. Twenty -"

"How soundly the child sleeps," Aunt Mary whispered, peeping in a little later to look at her niece. "These afternoon naps are the best thing in the world for her overworked little brain. I wish I could fill Chauncery with children, and let them run wild in the garden." She felt, not for the first time, how duty seemed to pull two ways at once, for there were many things she would fain have done had her duty to her mother not stood in the way.

Someone else came and looked at Mollie.

"Asleep!" Prudence exclaimed, with a smile. "Never mind, I can manage. It is getting very easy."

* * * * *

Mollie did not open her eyes the moment she woke up; she lay still, enjoying the warmth, the sweet scents, and the balmy air, so different from the cold winds of early spring. Presently she yawned, stretched herself like a sleepy kitten, and finally sat up and opened the lazy eyes.

"Good gracious!" she exclaimed, "Prue must have come and found me asleep. I wonder where she is."

She rose to her feet and looked about her as usual. She was in a place quite different from any she had seen hitherto. At her back stretched an orange-grove - there was no mistaking it, for the trees, planted evenly in rows, were laden with thousands of oranges, ripe and unripe, while the waxy white blossom with its golden heart still grew in clusters among the glossy dark leaves, sending its perfume out with the warm wind far and near. Before her, divided from the grove by a narrow, roughly fenced road, Mollie saw a wide, undulating plain, its surface covered somewhat scantily with coarse grass and occasional clumps of bracken. There were gum trees, large and small, their thin blue-green leaves hanging limply from the grey boughs, and throwing but little shade on the ground beneath. Some distance away a creek wound between wide banks of shingly sand and low boulders. At the nearer end a gum tree had fallen across the stream and had been left to form a crossing. Mollie thought it did not look a very inviting bridge to cross on a dark night.

Lydia Miller Middleton

It looked hot out there in the open. Mollie turned back to the orange-grove, cool and inviting, and had almost decided to explore in that direction, when the sound of voices fell upon her ear, and, turning again, she saw a group of children crossing the scrub land in front. In spite of wide hats and sunbonnets they were easily recognizable. The boys were walking in front and carried spades and pickaxes over their shoulders; the two girls were loitering along behind, and carried between them a large round article which might be a tub, a cradle, or a sieve. They were heading for the creek, and, as Mollie watched, Hugh lifted his hand and pointed towards the fallen log.

"Dick and Jerry are first to-day, and they have got over without any help from me," Mollie said to herself, with a tinge of jealousy, which, however, she quickly got rid of - jealousy not being part of a Girl Guide's equipment. She put her hands up to her mouth in the way she had seen the Australians do, and shouted "Cooo-eeeeeee!", with a creditably sustained shrill note at the end. Her call brought the children to a standstill, and they waited for her to join them.

"What are you going to do?" she asked.

"We are going to dig for gold," Prudence answered, as they started again. "Hugh says there is gold in the river-bed. The boys dig, and we sift the diggings in this cradle, which rocks in the water so that all the dirt runs out and the gold stays in - at least, it would if there were any to stay. Last year we dug for ever so long, but never got any gold at all. We found some pretty crystals, though."

"I found a purple one just like an amethyst," Grizzel

joined in; "but Mr. Fraser said it wasn't. Then I found a white one like a diamond, and a green one. I polished them with all my might, but I lost them except the green one. I hid it in a tree like the person who shot an arrow into the air, only my tree is a gum instead of an oak. I expect it is there still unbroke if it hasn't been stolen by a magpie or a blackie."

When they reached the creek the boys laid down their tools, and Hugh studied the lie of the land with an intent expression.

"We'll begin about here," he decided presently. "Last year we dug higher up, but I shouldn't wonder if gold silts downwards and collects in a hollow. This is about the hollowest place I have found yet. The soil in these old alluvial beds is often auriferous," he went on; "Mr. Fraser says this was once quite a respectable river, but years of dry seasons shrank it up. It will never go quite dry, because there is a good spring up there, and that is why he chose this place for his oranges. Irrigation is absolutely necessary for an orange-grove."

"Are we allowed to eat the oranges?" Dick asked anxiously, as a breath of scented wind blew across him.

"Oh yes - as many as we like. But we must dig first," Hugh replied firmly, lifting his spade as he spoke and planting it upright in the sandy soil. "First we must peg out our claims. There's a good deal of luck about gold-digging, of course, but you'd better look round and choose your own spot."

After some consideration the children decided to throw in their lot with Hugh, who was the only one among them who knew what gold looked like in its raw state.

"You can keep half and the rest of us will go shares in the other half," Dick suggested, quite forgetting in his interest that Time-travellers cannot carry profits with them on their travels. The plan sounded fair, however, so they agreed to it.

"It is possible that we may not find *gold*," Hugh said, as he marked out a square within which to begin operations; "but we are pretty sure to find something. Australian soil is extraordinarily rich in products. I should think it must be about the richest soil in the world."

"I hope it won't be ants," Prudence said nervously. "I do hate ants."

"Aunts!" exclaimed Jerry, not understanding Prue's Scottish-Australian pronunciation. "Why the dickens should we find aunts in a river-bed? Do they all drown themselves out here? Aunts can be jolly nice too - or jolly nasty, according to circs."

"They're *always* nasty here," Grizzel said emphatically, "I never met a nice ant in my life. They bite like red-hot nippers."

"Bite! Oh, I see," said Jerry, "you mean black aunts," vague memories of *Uncle Tom's Cabin* and Aunt Chloe floating in the back of his brain. "I thought you meant white aunts. I didn't know that aborigines were as fierce as all that."

"I have never seen any white ants here," said Prudence, who called the native Australians blacks when she spoke of them and a-borry-jines when she read about them. "Uncle Jim says there are a great many in India, and they eat his books."

Jerry looked bewildered. "Of course there's lots of 'em in India," he said, "but I never heard of them eating books."

"I expect your uncle means that they devour novels," suggested Mollie.

"No, he doesn't. He says they eat a tunnel through all his books from one end to the other. And they stuff up the keyholes."

"Your uncle's aunts must be quaint old birds then," Jerry said unbelievingly.

"But they aren't birds at all, they're *ants*," cried Grizzel.

A loud cackle from Hugh, whose grin had been growing wider and wider, now interrupted the discussion: "Ho, ho, ho! One of you is talking about aunts - your Aunt Maria - and the other is talking about ants - the beasts that go to the sluggard," he exploded. "You *are* a pair of muffs! He, he, he!"

"'Go to the ant, thou sluggard'," Mollie quoted slowly. "Oh - *Jerry* - "

It took them some time to recover from this little misunderstanding. "Next time I see Aunt Mary - bites like red-hot nippers - oh dear!"

"Well, come on and dig now," Hugh ordered at last, twisting a cord neatly round his last peg as he spoke.

"If you go on laughing like that you'll soon begin to cry, and this mine will never get started."

Thus adjured they rolled up their sleeves and set to work. Pickaxes were of no use in that sandy soil. The boys used their spades, and the girls carried the turned-up sand to the creek, washing it with the utmost care in the cinder-sifter. But their efforts met with no success. Neither gold nor anything else, except pebbles, rewarded their toil.

"It's always like that," Hugh said at last, sitting down on the edge of the hole they had dug. "Gold is the most gambly stuff imaginable. We know a lady who was as poor as a washerwoman one day, and then at breakfast one morning she got a letter to say her goldmine shares had struck a reef, and she got so rich she simply didn't know what to do with her money. She came to see Papa about it. She was an old maid, so naturally there wasn't much she wanted. You never know who is going to be rich and who poor, with a goldmine. Some of these pebbles are quite valuable," he continued, running a handful of shingle through his fingers, "there are amethysts and opals and topazes in some river beds. I have never found one myself, but I've picked up some pretty good crystals."

"I think I'll go and look for mine," said Grizzel. "I hid it in a tree near here. I am tired of gold-digging, and my feet are hot. I shall dabble them in the creek and eat an orange."

She got up as she spoke and went off towards a particularly gaunt-looking tree. Its trunk had split open, showing a hollow large enough to hold several people; for some distance around its roots protruded through the ground like old bones. Grizzel disappeared into the hollow trunk, whence she presently emerged with an air of triumph. "I've got it safe and sound. Now I'm going to get an orange."

Jerry eyed the orange-grove lovingly. Digging is thirsty work.

"Let's all go," said Hugh. "Orange juice is one of the most restorative things in the world; if we eat enough we will be ready to make a fresh start in half an hour or so. Very likely we shall have better luck next time."

It was hot, and the change from the glaring sunshine into the cool dampness of the orange-grove was very pleasant. The beautiful fruit hung invitingly from the branches with a colour and fragrance unknown to London shops. There were many varieties, and the Australian children wandered critically from tree to tree.

"I'm not sure whether I like navels or bloods best," Hugh remarked, "but perhaps on the whole, for pure refreshment, navels."

He stopped, as he spoke, before a tree on which grew oranges larger than the London children had ever seen in their lives - immense, smooth, opulent-looking globes of rich golden yellow. For a time silence reigned, while six people covered themselves with juice, "Like the ointment that ran down Aaron's beard," Grizzel said, and the ground in the neighbourhood assumed an auriferous hue that made the inventor sigh.

"I wish we could find a place where nuggets lay about like that , " he said rather pensively ; " it would be awfully jolly."

"It would be," agreed the others, "most awfully jolly."

"I think I'd as soon have oranges as gold," Grizzel said reflectively, looking down at the peel-strewn earth. "Think how nice it would be if you were in the very middle of a scorching desert, and dying of thirst like the men in *Five Weeks in a Balloon*, to find a lovely orange tree covered with juicy oranges. It would be nicer than finding gold."

"You do talk silly slithers," Hugh said derisively. "Who ever found a beautiful orange tree in the middle of a desert? You *might* find gold and bribe an Arab to give you water."

"You *might* find an orange tree in an oasis," Grizzel said huffily. "I am going to bathe my feet in the creek. Go and look for your old gold. You won't find it."

"All right, Carroty-cross-patch. You won't get any if we do," Hugh replied politely.

"Don't want it, Goggle-eyed-guinea-pig." Grizzel got up and walked off, her sun-bonnet dangling down her back and her red curls waving over her head. No one took any notice of these little amenities. No one remembered that the ointment which ran down Aaron's beard was like brethren dwelling together in unity - a good and pleasant thing. They were all brothers or sisters and accustomed to such mellifluous modes of address.

"We'd better go back and dig in a new place," said Hugh; "the light will begin to fade before very long."

They gathered up their orange peel and buried it tidily, and then stepped out of the cool grove into the hot sunshine with some reluctance. But gold-digging is not mere play, as Hugh reminded them. If you want to find a large nugget you begin by looking for small ones, and the search undoubtedly entails some hard work.

The new diggings were no more productive than the old. The boys worked industriously, digging widely rather than deeply. It was decidedly monotonous work, and Dick began to think that for pure excitement gold-digging showed up poorly beside football. Their backs ached, their hands were blistered, and the shingly pebbles got into their shoes. They were hot and thirsty, and into the minds of four of them crept a suspicion that Grizzel had chosen the better way of spending the time. They could see her sitting on a boulder, her feet in the water and her hands occupied with her crystal, which she was rubbing in a leisurely way on a stone, as one sharpens slate-pencils. The afternoon wore on; the sun seemed to gain in speed as he slanted down the sky, and tree shadows lay about the ground like long thin skeletons. A herd of cows, on their way to the milking-shed, trailed lazily past the weary diggers, reminding them of tea-time with its refreshing drinks and soothing cream and butter.

Jerry stood up, dropping his spade and stretching his arms above his head.

"I'm tired," he announced. "Let's hang our spades on a gummy tree and sit beside Carrots for a bit. I'd like to dabble my little feet too, before walking home."

Hugh assented somewhat reluctantly; he would have preferred to continue digging while daylight lasted.

"We've done *something*," he said, as they took off their shoes and stockings; "we've found where gold isn't, and that's rather important."

"I know lots of places where it isn't," said Dick, putting his hands in his pockets, "I could have told you that without digging for a whole afternoon, if I'd known it was important."

"Of course I mean when it isn't where it might be," Hugh amended, taking no notice of Dick's gibe. "It's what Papa calls the process of elimination. You've got to do it with almost everything worth having really. You've only got to look at this river bed to see there's pretty sure to be something worth having there - in fact I know there is. It may not be gold, but it's something."

"How do you know it?" Mollie asked curiously. "I don't see anything particular about the river bed. It doesn't look half so likely as the gold patch in the road beside your cherry garden."

"I can't tell you how, but I do. Just you wait and see. To-morrow I think I'll try the old place again. I shall go on trying till I find something, either gold or precious stones. There might even be diamonds; there are in some river beds."

"Look," said Grizzel, holding out her hand with the stone in it, "I have rubbed a bit off one side at last. If I rub long enough it will come bright all over."

A small, roughly eight-sided crystal lay in the palm of her hand. Six sides were dull and colourless, the remaining two sides were clear and transparent.

"I rubbed my bit off exactly opposite the bit that was clean already," she went on, "so that I could look through it at the sun." She turned the crystal over and held it up as she spoke. A dazzling flash of pale-green light darted out, as though an unearthly finger were pointing at the sun. It was gone in a moment, and the stone looked dull and rough as before.

"What was that?" Grizzel asked, in a startled voice. "Is it going to go off like fireworks?"

"Give it to me," said Hugh, taking it from Grizzel's unresisting fingers. He held it up as she had done, and again the pale-green light flashed out. He moved it slightly from side to side, and with his movements the green light took on the shining hues of a rainbow.

"It's like a diamond," said Prudence in an awed voice.

"It *is* a diamond," cried Hugh. "I knew it! I knew it! I said so! Grizzel found it in the place we dug last year. Grizzel found it, but it was me that looked for it, because I knew! Where this one was there will be more. *We have found a diamond bed!*"

"If Grizzel hadn't rubbed it so hard you would never have known," Prudence reminded him. "She rubbed that bit for *weeks* last year."

Hugh turned the crystal over and over, examining it on every side. "Diamonds are terrifically hard," he explained more calmly. "It takes months to cut and polish a diamond properly. Grizzel's pretty good at sticking to a thing; I'll say that for her. I'm glad the first diamond was found by her."

"Well - it will take me some time to polish it all over," Grizzel said, with a sigh. "If I did nothing else all day long but rub it on a stone it would be clean in about six months."

"Who does this land belong to?" Jerry asked. "Is it your father's?"

"Oh, no - it's Mr. Eraser's. For miles around the land is his. That's the man we are staying with."

"Then the diamond is Mr. Fraser's, not yours or Grizzel's," Jerry pronounced.

There was a short silence. "Mr. Fraser said I might have all the gold I found," Hugh said, in a doubtful tone.

"I expect he guessed that you wouldn't find any," Jerry responded. "But a diamond like that is a different thing. If it really is a diamond it is probably pretty valuable - perhaps it is worth a hundred pounds. You can't walk off with a hundred pounds without telling."

"Well, we'll show it to him. Of course we'll tell him we have found a diamond bed," Hugh answered.

"It's my diamond," Grizzel declared. "I found it and I rubbed it and it slept under my pillow, and I hid it and I love it and it's mine. I don't care what anybody says."

"Mr. Fraser will most likely give you lots of money for it," Mollie suggested soothingly, "and then you can go and buy something nicer than a diamond."

"I don't want lots of money. I want my own dear little

stone that I rubbed myself," Grizzel repeated, tears starting to her eyes. "Why should Mr. Fraser take my stone and chop it all up with horrible sharp grinding knives? It's mine. I found it."

"You'll have to show it to him first," Hugh said decisively, "whether you found it or not. If you keep it you will be a thief, and perhaps you will be sent to prison."

"Then I'd rather let it go back to its home in the river bed," Grizzel cried passionately. As she spoke she snatched the crystal from Hugh's hand; there was a flash of green light - a splash - and it was gone.

She turned and ran, sobbing and crying. Prudence followed, bent upon comforting her. Mollie looked scared, Jerry laughed, Hugh shrugged his shoulders:

"Just like a girl!" he said. "It doesn't matter; we'll find more. But that was a good diamond; I'd have liked to show it to Mr. Fraser. We'd better collect our things and go home."

Three of them turned away, but Dick lingered behind. His quick eyes, trained to watching the flight of balls of all sizes from footballs to golf-balls, had taken accurate note of the spot where that little splash had been. There were still circles widening round it. The creek looked shallow just there.

"If I scooped up the sand carefully *now*, as likely as not I'd retrieve that stone," he said to himself. "Grizzel is a decent little kid; she'll be sorry by and by, and, besides, the old chap ought to have his diamond if it really is a diamond. Diamonds aren't so jolly easy to come by as

Hugh seems to think. That white stone is almost in the middle of the circle - I'll make for that."

"Don't wait for me," he shouted after the others, "I'm coming in a jiff." He waited till he saw them turn their somewhat dejected and preoccupied backs upon the scene of the late disaster, and then transferred his attention to the creek. At the point where he stood the water was comparatively deep; it had evidently formed a channel for itself, helped, probably, by a slender waterfall which dropped over a large boulder on the higher ground some distance beyond the fallen tree.

"I can crawl over that and drop off at the shallow part," he thought, "I'll have to look sharp or the circles will be gone."

He rolled up his already short flannels and started. The tree was by no means steady - it rolled and shook under his weight; but, as the worst that could happen would be a good soaking, he did not worry overmuch, and soon slid off into the shallow stream. As he had predicted, the water there barely reached to his knees. He scrutinized the ever-widening circle, now faint and irregular, and, calculating the distance from its edge to its centre, he fixed his eyes intently upon the white stone and cautiously waded towards it, his movements in the water breaking up the last traces of the circle. When he reached the white stone he halted.

"It was here, almost to a T, or my name is not Richard Gordon," he muttered, and, stooping carefully, he scooped up a double handful of shingly sand from the river bottom. He stood up, letting the water run away through his tightly closed fingers. As he bent his head to examine the pebbles left in his hand, a sunbeam darted over his shoulder - there was a flash of pale green.

"Got it, by jinks!" he chuckled exultantly. "First go-off! Good for you, Richard, my boy - your eye is pretty well in and no mistake. Come out of that, my young diamond, and let's have a look at you - you'd do A1 for heliographing with."

Dick soon scrambled to shore, and stood for a moment looking after the others, now far ahead. "I'll put him back in the hollow trunk where Grizzel hid him," he decided, with a twinkle in his eyes. "It might be rather a lark -"

A sharp sprint brought him up with the other two boys, who were awaiting his arrival seated on the top of a slip-rail, Mollie having gone in search of Prudence and Grizzel.

"What on earth have you been doing?" Hugh demanded. "Have you been swimming?"

"I was only having a look round," Dick answered, with a wink at Jerry; "I thought I'd do a little prospecting on my own."

"Why didn't you tell me, you beast?" Jerry asked, linking his arm into Dick's affectionately.

Dick answered by a friendly punch on the head. "Who is Mr. Fraser?" he asked Hugh, settling himself in his place on the rail.

"He is a man we know," Hugh replied rather vaguely. "He owns all this part and is as rich as a nabob, but he isn't married, so he lives up here all alone, with two or three Chinese servants in the house. He once lived in China. He's awfully fond of gardening, and pictures, and that sort of thing, like my mater. He's a merchant and he owns ships. He's a great friend of the pater's, and he comes in about once a week to hear the mater sing, and they yarn away about home and spout poetry. But he is quite a jolly sort of chap when you get him alone. His house is called Drink Between, which wouldn't be a bad name for a book if you wanted to write one."

"Jolly good name for a pub, if you wanted to keep one," Jerry remarked. "I shouldn't wonder if he got it from some old coaching inn of the olden times - though, of course, we are in the olden times already, if it comes to that - fairly old, at any rate."

"No, he got it from a place at home where Prince Charlie once had a drink. When the girls are here he gets in a couple of women to look after them. Other times he only has his heathen Chinee lot, and jolly good they are! That is, of course, if you like stewed puppy and bird's nest," Hugh added solemnly; "I love 'em myself."

"Adore 'em," Jerry said, smacking his lips. "Never lose a chance of having puppy-tail hash when we can get it, do we, old son?"

"Rather not," Dick replied. "Remember those bird's-nest tarts our old woman at the tuck-shop used to make before butter got so scarce? Scrumptious!"

The appearance of the girls interrupted these flights of masculine fancy. Grizzel still looked subdued, but the tears were dried, and she was listening politely to Mollie's tuneful advice to "Pack your troubles in your own kit-bag, and smile, smile, smile". Hugh shouted to them to hurry up or they would be late for tea, and soon the little party was under way again, as cheerful as if diamonds had never been heard of. They were now in sight of Drink Between; a square, solidly built house, with a wide veranda and balcony on three sides of it, completely hidden at present under a pale-purple drapery of wistaria.

"It looks like an amethyst," Mollie said admiringly, as they drew near. "I never saw such a purple house as that before."

The inside of Drink Between was entirely different from any of the other Australian houses which Mollie had been in. They entered by a side door which opened straight on to a narrow stairway. The girls climbed up to their bedroom, a large airy apartment opening on to the balcony.

"Where are your father and mother and Baby?" Mollie asked, as they washed away the remains of oranges and gold-digging.

"Papa and Mamma have to go and meet an immigrant ship to-morrow, so they aren't coming up till afterwards. And Baby and Bridget are with them."

"What's an immigrant ship?" asked Mollie.

"A ship full of immigrants," Prudence replied, brushing out her curls with conscientious care. "Immigrants are people who get their passage out for nothing, or for very little, and then they go to work here. Mamma is getting a new cook because ours is going to be married. And Papa likes to meet the Scotch immigrants and say welcome to Australia to them. Bridget was an immigrant, but she says she will soon be Australian."

"I see," said Mollie thoughtfully. "Are they ever married? I mean - do children come with their parents?"

"Yes, lots of them. Are you ready, Mollie? The boys are getting impatient. I can hear them growling."

Feeling very fresh and clean in white muslin frocks with pale-blue sashes, the girls descended by a different and much wider staircase than the one they had gone up by. They stepped off the stairs straight into a large hall, or living-room, which apparently occupied half the floor of the house, for on two sides it opened on to the veranda, and on the third side into a large bamboo house; the fourth wall was unbroken but for one door. The room was painted white, and the floor covered with fine white Chinese matting, over which lay a few Eastern rugs, their once rich and glowing colours now dimmed by time and the tread of generations of feet. Through the wide-open French windows could be seen the long, graceful streamers of wistaria, hanging from the arched boughs round the veranda like a lace veil. Against this background grew masses of pale-pink and blue hydrangeas, with their flat fragile flowers and broad leaves. The bamboo house was given wholly to ferns, over which a fountain was playing, and under the fine spray the green fronds glistened as freshly as though they grew in the heart of an English wood.

The sun was now setting, and its crimson glow shone

through the mauve wistaria, filling the room with an opal-coloured light which made Mollie think of fairyland. It fell with a peculiarly pleasant effect upon a round tea-table spread for tea. She had never seen such fine and snowy damask, such shining silver, or such delicately transparent china cups and saucers. Even Grannie's well-kept table paled before the exquisite freshness of this one. As for the food part - there was a crystal bowl of yellow clotted cream, a plate of gossamer balls which were probably intended to pass for scones, a twist of gold which was most likely meant for bread, and dishes of preserves unknown to the English children - tiny green oranges in syrup, scarlet rose-berries, and jellies like amber and topaz, looking as though some of Hugh's precious stones had been cooked for his tea.

They were about half-way through this beautiful meal when there was a sound of footsteps on the matting, and a Chinese servant appeared, bearing a large iced birthday cake set on a silver tray.

"Hullo, Ah Kew! What you gottee there?" called Hugh, under the impression that he was speaking pidgin-English to perfection.

"Master talkee to-day b'long he burfday," Ah Kew replied. "He talkee my, wanchee cook makee one piecee burfday-cake." He set the cake down in front of Prudence as he spoke.

"Welly good, Ah Kew, Master b'long quitey righty," said Hugh approvingly. "Cook makee jolly-good cakee, me eat jolly-good cakee. Cook pleased, me pleased, cakee pleased, all jolly-welly pleased."

Ah Kew smiled a slow and mysterious smile, his black eyes closing up under his slanting eyebrows, and his blue-capped head nodding. He glanced over the tea-table.

"Tea b'long all plopper?" he asked anxiously. "S'pose you wanchee more can have plenty more."

"No, thank you, Ah Kew, me eatee more me bustee," Hugh replied politely. Ah Kew nodded his head again and departed, his pigtail flapping against the long skirts of his blue cotton coat.

Prudence cut the beautiful cake and distributed large slices all round. No grown-up person was present to make sensible remarks about not eating too much, which was a good or a bad thing "according to circs" as Jerry would say.

The children were all tired after their hard work and excitement; Mr. Fraser was not coming home till late, and had left a message to say that he expected to find everyone fast asleep in bed when he got back; so, after a tour of exploration round the house and its immediate neighbourhood, they went off to their rooms, and soon most of them were asleep.

Not all of them, however. Whether it was the cake, or the change of air, or the strange bed, or still stranger circumstances, or all combined, it would be hard to say, but it seemed to Dick that the longer he lay in bed the more wakeful he became. The thought of the diamond began to worry him, and soon assumed gigantic proportions in his mind. Suppose it got lost. Perhaps it was worth a hundred pounds, as Jerry had suggested. Suppose a magpie flew off with it. It might be worth more than a hundred; perhaps two hundred pounds. What if a blackfellow stole it, or the tree fell down in the night, or got burnt up. It is true that none of these things had happened during the months in which it had lain there before, but *then* no one had known that it was valuable. It would be just like luck, or rather unluck, if something happened this particular night. Dick's knowledge of diamonds was so small that it could be hardly said to exist, and he now began to have nightmarish visions of huge sums of money - thousands of pounds perhaps, lost through his folly. To be sure, no one knew that he had put the diamond back in the tree. But he knew himself, which was the main thing. He tossed from side to side restlessly. A new thought perplexed him. How could anything he did or left undone matter now, seeing that he wasn't going to be born for another thirty years? He belonged to the future, and the future could not influence the present - at least, he supposed not, but funny things did happen. Anyhow, this was *his* present for the moment, and he had his usual irritating conscience.

He got out of bed at last and went to the window. There was such a flood of moonlight that out-of-doors was almost as light as day. Why not slip into his clothes and scoot down to the bottom of the scrub-land, and collect that diamond? It would be better than tossing about in bed, and afterwards he would go calmly to sleep. The difficulty would be to get out of the house. Probably Ah Kew was on the watch for his master, and, if he saw Dick, would remark "no can do", or words to that effect.

Dick went to the edge of the balcony and looked over; it was not very far from the ground, but it was too far to jump. How about the wistaria boughs? They looked pretty tough - he decided to try, and if he fell - well, he had smashed himself up before this more than once, and no doubt would do so again. A few tumbles more or less wouldn't make much difference to him, especially, he reflected, as he was bound to get back to 1920 somehow or other. He could hardly kill himself now if he tried.

He reached the ground with nothing worse than a few scratches to his credit, and set off along the path by which they had come in the afternoon, keeping well in the shadow of the hedge in case Ah Kew's beady eyes should be on the outlook. So long as he was within the grounds of the house he felt confident and cheerful, but when he reached the slip-rail and looked over into the land beyond he felt some of his courage oozing away.

It looked eerie, that strange, unfamiliar country, in this white light. There were dead trees standing here and there, and their pale trunks took unpleasant shapes - they might conceivably be something else than trees - not ghosts, of course; there were no such things as ghosts. All the tales he had ever read about Australia suddenly started up in his mind - tales of deadly snakes, of bushrangers, of blackfellows, who had methods of their own of doing you in. One might go through a good deal without being actually *killed*. Now that he came to think of it, Australia in the 'seventies was a wildish sort of place - in some parts at any rate. He wished that he was surer where he was - how far away from civilization. He supposed that Ned Kelly and his gang were still at large.

But, of course, he could not go back. He stepped cautiously from tree to tree, keeping to the black shadows as much as possible. He could hear the sound of that little waterfall quite distinctly, and see the moonlight on the rippling shallows of the creek - now he could see the gum tree he was making for - he had taken particular notice of a crooked bough - what on earth was that?

A wild piercing shriek from somewhere beyond the creek brought him suddenly to a standstill, his heart in his mouth. Undoubtedly a woman was being murdered or tortured. Blackfellows, probably, as Ned Kelly made a point of not hurting women - at least so it said in *Robbery Under Arms*. Dick wondered what exactly the blackfellows had done to the woman - and there was the blood-curdling shriek again!

He stood still. After all, why not leave the diamond till daylight? He had been a silly ass to imagine all that rubbish about it, and a much sillier ass to leave his safe bedroom and come out to this wild and desolate spot all alone. If he had brought Jerry -

Ah, Jerry! There had been that affair of Jerry's eldest brother and the guns. Ten wounds. Both legs shot off. "Stick it out, you chaps." The very last words he spoke in this world, sweeter in Jerry's ear, Dick knew, than the finest poetry ever written. He gathered himself together and went on. It would never do to begin a habit of *not* sticking it out. For, wherever he was, he was always Dick Gordon to himself - a person for whom he wished to have a considerable amount of respect.

He wished that the orange grove, so cool and lovely by day, did not look so dark and mysterious by night.

At last ! Here was the old tree. Now for it. He stepped

round, prepared to enter the empty hollow regardless of possible snakes or blacks, when he heard a sound that made the hair rise on his head and the back of his neck feel queer, for it was unmistakably a child crying inside the tree. The child of the murdered woman, he thought. So the blacks *were* near - perhaps inside the tree at this very moment. The idea flitted across his mind that there was an extraordinary difference between reading about a thing and experiencing it. As the child's sobs continued he shrunk together - he would rather meet an enemy in the open and be shot at twenty times than face these savage and mysterious blacks - and then he suddenly decided that, if there were a child there, he must go and look for it and do his best, blacks or no blacks.

But at that very instant the crying stopped and turned to speaking:

"Please, God, let there be a miracle. Just this once, God. I'm sorry, God; I'll be good if you'll make a miracle. Only this once. I am very, very sorry." The crying began again.

"Grizzel!" exclaimed Dick, his fears all vanishing like darkness before light. "How on earth did she get there? She'll be frightened into fits if she sees me." He moved back a little distance and stopped to think. The best plan would be to call her softly, he decided.

"Grizzel! Where are you, Grizzel? Are you there, kiddy? It's Dick calling. Are you in your tree? I'm coming - look out!"

He came up to the hollow opening and looked in. It was Grizzel sure enough, in her little dressing-gown, her face blotched with tears and her curls crushed and tumbled. Dick put an arm round her: "Don't cry, kiddy; the diamond is all right."

"Oh, Dick, I did hope there might be a miracle," she sobbed, burying her head on his shoulder. "I'm so sorry. My poor little diamond, all those years and years shut up in the ground! It had just one look at the sun and then I threw it back. Oh, Dick, if God would only make a miracle this *once* and put my diamond back!"

Dick felt a choky sensation in his throat as the thin little arm tightened round his neck.

"It's all right, Grizzel," he whispered, "we'll find the diamond - let my arm loose a moment." He groped round, and in another minute the stone was in his hand. He turned it over, and a pale-green ray darted out, more unearthly than ever in the moonlight.

Grizzel gave a cry as he laid it on her palm. "My diamond! The miracle! I *thought* it would happen! I just *thought* God hadn't forgotten the way! Oh, Dick, I am so glad! I am so glad! My own dear little diamond!"

Dick had not the heart to explain at the moment that there had been no miracle, and Grizzel was far too preoccupied with her own joy and relief to wonder what had brought Dick to her tree just then; and besides, he thought vaguely, one never knows.

"We must be going in," he said; "it's ever so late and we'll be cotched. How on earth did you get out?"

"Down the back stairs. The others were asleep, but I

could not sleep, thinking of my little diamond in the cold river -" at that moment a wild shriek rang out again, and Dick started violently.

"It's only a curlew calling to his friend," Grizzel said, creeping out of the hollow. "They scream exactly like people being killed, but it's only their way; they mean to be kind."

Dick drew a long breath. A wild bird and a crying child! Suppose he had gone back! Thank goodness he hadn't, but it was a near shave.

The boy and girl walked happily along, hand in hand. They had reached the slip-rail and were climbing over, when a tall man appeared from the garden of Drink Between.

"*Grizzel!* What in the wide creation are you doing here at this hour of night, or rather morning? Do you know it is nearly one o'clock? And what are you doing, young man?"

"Oh, Mr. Fraser - it's Mr. Fraser," she explained, turning to Dick, and such a confused tale followed, in which crystals, gold-mines, diamonds, wickedness, and miracles were all jumbled together, that Mr. Fraser decided that a glass of milk, a biscuit, and bed, had better pave the way to a fuller explanation next day.

Ah Kew let them in with a wise smile and several nods of his head, and soon both Dick and Grizzel were sleeping as soundly as the other four Time-travellers.

"It is a green diamond," Mr. Fraser pronounced next morning, "but what its value is we cannot tell until it is cut and polished. Then it will belong to Grizzel, to have and to hold till death do them part. If you really have found a diamond-mine, youngsters, something will have to be done about shares. Who finds keeps, you know. We'll have the place properly surveyed and see what happens. But don't begin counting your chickens too soon - these Australian diamond-mines are tricksy things; you never know how they are going to pan out. Wait a bit before you plan what to do with your fortune."

Mollie, Dick, and Jerry suddenly felt very sad as they remembered that they were out of this stroke of luck. Whatever happened, Fortune was not preparing to smile on *them*, at least not in a way that would be of any immediate practical use to them when they got back to London. And a fortune apiece would have come in so very handy just now - just forty years hence, that is. The boys made up their minds to investigate this matter of fortunes in the colonies directly they got home.

Hugh tossed up his hat and caught it again: "We'll be jolly rich," he cried. "The Mater will get her trip home, and the Pater needn't worry about bills and subscription lists any more, and I'll get that camera - oh, 'hard times, hard times, come again no more!'"

*　*　*　*　*

Mollie sat up. The clock was still ticking minutes into hours, hours into days, days into weeks and months and years.

"Oh dear," she said, "I do wonder -"

"Wonder what, my Molliekins?" asked Aunt Mary, preceding Hester with the tea-tray.

"I wonder," Mollie repeated, and then began to laugh. "I don't suppose you ever bit like red-hot nippers, did you, Aunt Mary?"

CHAPTER VI

The Grape-Gatherers or Who was Mr. Smith?

Aunt Mary had gone up to London to do some shopping, and when Mollie came downstairs next morning she found Grannie installed in the drawing-room, instead of in the morning-room as usual, with another old lady who had come to spend the day.

"Mrs. Pell and I were at school together," she explained, as she introduced her grandchild, "and that was not yesterday," she added, as she settled Mollie in an easy-chair with the lame foot up on a cushioned frame. "My dear husband used this when he had gout," she continued, tucking a warm shawl round Mollie's bandages and large bedroom slipper. "It was made in the village under his own directions, and is most ingeniously constructed. Poor, dear Richard was such an active man; he could not endure to lie on a sofa, and I had the greatest difficulty in keeping him to his bed even when his attacks were severe."

Mrs. Pell shook her head as she looked admiringly at the foot-rest. "James was the same, he hated a sofa and would always sit in a chair. Not that he was so active, but he was stout, and stout people are more comfortable sitting up than lying on their backs."

Mollie coughed. She had either to cough or to laugh, which, of course, would never have done.

"My dear, I trust you have not caught cold," Grannie said anxiously. "Perhaps we should close the window. Your Aunt Mary has a perfect craze for open windows, and I sometimes think there is a draught in this room."

"No, no, Grannie," Mollie protested; "I have not got the least bit of cold, and I love the open window; it is so warm to-day. It was only a tickle; I get them some-times - tell me about when you and Mrs. Pell were at school, please."

The two old ladies smiled at each other over their spectacles.

"That was not yesterday," Grannie repeated. "You would think very poorly of our school. We had no games, no gym-dress, no examinations such as you have; but we learnt the use of the globes very thoroughly, and we spoke French, so that we were not at a loss when we went to Paris later on. Our dancing was much more graceful than the foolish gambols with their ridiculous titles which you young people call dancing nowadays. Fox-trot, indeed! And bunny-hug. And rag-time. I never heard such names in my life! *We* danced the Highland schottische, and the quadrille, and Sir Roger de Coverley. And do you remember your famous curtsy, Esther? And how Madame made you show off on parents' day?"

"Indeed I do!" Mrs. Pell answered briskly. "I believe I could do it now, this moment. I have been wonderfully free of rheumatism this year."

"Do, do," Mollie begged, overlooking the insult to her beloved fox-trot in her anxiety to see a real old-fashioned curtsy.

Mrs. Pell laid her knitting on one side, rose from her chair, and walked to the middle of the room. She shook her somewhat ample black silk skirt into place, tilted her chin to an angle that gave her a decidedly haughty expression, and stood facing Grannie and Mollie.

"You must imagine yourselves to be our beloved Queen Victoria and our beautiful and gracious Alexandra, Princess of Wales," she said, looking so elegant and distinguished that Mollie suddenly felt rather small and shy, while Grannie, on the other hand, drew herself up into what was presumably the attitude of Her late Majesty.

Mrs. Pell lifted her skirts with an easy turn of her pretty hands and wrists, pointed a charming foot, so small that it made Mollie gasp, and began to sink slowly down. Down, down, down she swept, her skirt billowing out around her, her shoulders square, her head erect - down till she all but touched the floor, and how she kept her balance was a perfect miracle; then slowly up, with an indescribably graceful curve of neck and elbows, till once more she stood erect, pleased and triumphant, a pretty pink flush on her cheeks.

Grannie clapped her hands. "There, Miss Mollie! That was how *we* were taught to curtsy! There's nothing resembling a fox about *that*!" she exclaimed, as Mrs. Pell took her seat again and resumed her knitting.

"It was perfectly lovely," Mollie agreed warmly, "but it

Lydia Miller Middleton

does require the right kind of skirt, Grannie. Did anyone ever topple over at the critical moment?"

"Not that I can remember," Mrs. Pell answered; "but, of course, it required a great deal of practice, and we did many exercises before we got the length of our court curtsy. Do you remember Ellen Bathurst, Daisy?" (How funny it sounded to hear Grannie called Daisy.) "And the time all the brandy-balls fell out of her pocket? *How* angry Madame was!"

Of course Mollie had to hear about the adventure of the brandy-balls, and from that the talk drifted to memories of old friends long since dead and gone, whose names Mollie had never heard. It was a little depressing, and her thoughts wandered away to the Campbells. She wondered where she would find herself that afternoon, and then remembered with dismay that Aunt Mary was away and there would be no tunes.

But after lunch Grannie insisted upon the sofa as usual. "You shall have your lullaby," she said. "Mrs. Pell and I are going to play duets. We used to play a great deal together when we were young, and no doubt our music is just the thing for sending you to sleep; it has a base and a treble and some perfectly distinct tunes."

"Don't be sarcastic, Grannie," Mollie laughed, as Grannie bent to kiss her. "I am sure it is beautiful music, and I like tunes myself. Jean is the musical one of our family. She jiggles up and down the piano in no particular key and calls it 'The Scent of Lilac on a June Day'."

" Well, well ," said Grannie. "Times change. We are

going to play selections from *Faust*, with variations. Sleep quietly till tea-time, my dear."

Mollie smiled as she listened to the selections. "- two-three, *one*-two-three, *one* -" she could hear the treble counting. "I like it," she murmured to herself rather sleepily - the morning's conversation had not been exciting on her side. "I am glad I am not James, for this is an awfully comfortable sofa - hullo, Prue! You *are* in a hurry to-day! I was just thinking of a nap -"

Prudence did not answer; she was listening to the piano.

"Mamma sings that," she said. "It's *Faust*. I adore *Faust*. Don't you? The waltz simply makes my feet go wild."

"I don't know it," Mollie confessed. "There are so many things I don't know. Hurry up, Prue. I have had such an aged morning; now I want a young afternoon."

"- two-three, *one*-two-three, *one* -" said Prue, taking Mollie's hand in her own.

* * * * *

It was very hot. So hot that Mollie could not be bothered to move. She was half-sitting, half-lying on a bed of bracken, and around her she could see the supine forms of four other children - Prudence and Grizzel, Dick and Jerry - all lying in various attitudes of exhaustion and apparently all asleep. Mollie was too lazy to turn her head, but she could see that they were in a wood. The trees were the eternal gum trees, with their monotonous grey trunks and perpetual blue-green

Lydia Miller Middleton

foliage. They were not growing in the neighbourly manner of trees in an English wood, nor did they throw the cool green shade of elms and beeches, but still in their own way they formed a wood. Mollie lay with her back propped up against one of the grey trunks, her arms behind her head, and her eyes blinking sleepily. She wondered where Hugh was.

"You *are* a lazy lot," said a voice behind her. "I have been helping in the vineyards all morning, and I've discovered a new kind of grape. Mr. von Greusen thinks it might turn out to be a good champagne grape. The carts are coming down; don't you want to see them?"

As he spoke Hugh came round and stood at Mollie's side. He wore a coat of tussore silk, and his shirt was open at the neck; a wide pith helmet was on his head, draped with a striped pugaree with broad ends hanging down his back, and further decorated with vine leaves, which looked rather droopy in the heat. He held out a hand to Mollie and pulled her up, looking scornfully at the recumbent figures of Jerry and Dick.

"What a way to spend the time!" he exclaimed. "Their eyes tight shut and their legs spread out like dried fruit. *They'll* never discover a new grape and have the most famous champagne in the world called after them. Come on!"

Mollie had been listening for a little while to a distant rumble. It now resolved itself into the uneven racketty grind of heavy cart-wheels on a rough track. She went forward with Hugh, and, shading her eyes from the glare of the sun, looked up the road which wound between the trees of the wood they were in. As she watched, the carts came into view round a bend of the track, and soon they were passing before her. A team of six oxen drew each heavy load - such a load as Mollie had never seen in her life. Grapes! Grapes piled up like turnips! They had been thrown in by careless hands accustomed to working with rich harvests, and here and there they hung over the sides, or dropped to the ground, to be trodden under foot by indifferent beasts and weary men.

The noise of trampling feet and creaking wheels disturbed the sleepers, who, one by one, got up and came beside Mollie and Hugh. There was a smell of hot grapes in the air, mingled with the smell of sweating oxen, dry grass, and pungent eucalyptus, and the spilled juice of grapes mixing with the hot dust of the track added a peculiar aroma of its own to the general nosegay, as Dick described it. Mollie thought that she could never remember smelling anything so thirst-inducing in all her days. When the last cart had disappeared down the winding road, and the noisy rattle had died away to a distant rumble again, Hugh sat down on the trunk of a fallen tree and stretched his arms.

"Where are they going?" asked Dick, now wideawake and curious. "What happens next?"

"They're going to Mr. von Greusen's place to be made into wine," Hugh answered, "and it's a funny thing that however nice grapes are raw they are all equally nasty when turned into wine. Some go sour and black and you call it claret, and some go sharp and yellow and you call it Frontignac or any other silly yellow name. What *I* should like to invent would be a kind of drink that tasted of grapes, fresh sweet grapes. I'd add a dash of peach, and a slice or two of melon, and a bottle of soda-water. And just enough powdered sugar. And ice."

"Let's go and get the things now and make it this very minute," said Grizzel, tying on her sun-bonnet and making ready to start. "I'm *so* thirsty."

"It's too late to-day, and besides I'm tired. There was a man up there who wanted to know all sorts of things about the vineyards. Mr. von Greusen was too busy to go round with him, so he sent me. He was pleased with me for discovering that grape. The man's name is John Smith. I think he is French."

Mollie laughed.

"What are you laughing at?" asked Hugh, looking all ready to be offended.

"Oh - nothing - I'm not laughing," Mollie declared; "it's only a sort of tickle; I get it sometimes."

"John Smith isn't exactly a French name," said Jerry. "Why do you think he is French?"

"Because he called Mr. von Greusen a 'vigneron' and talked about 'hectares' instead of acres, and 'hectolitres' instead of gallons, and he told me how vines were trained in Champagne and Burgundy and Languedoc - all very Frenchy. Mr. von Greusen never talks like that. He was interested in my new grape, but he's afraid it won't go on being like it is now. He says it has about one chance in a hundred. I don't mind betting you sixpence it *will* be a champagne grape."

"I don't mind betting you sixpence he isn't French if his name is John Smith," said Jerry. "You might as well call yourself a Scotsman named Chung Li Chang."

"Oh - names! Names are nothing out here," Hugh said loftily. "We can call ourselves what we please. This is the Land of Liberty. Besides, Papa knows a Scotsman called Devereux, so there you are."

"Faugh!" said Jerry scornfully. "That's nothing! Everyone knows that Scotland is full of French names."

"I suppose you are trying to say 'sfaw'," said Hugh coldly. "There is nothing to sfaw about. Lots of Chinese people come to Australia and call themselves John Smith if they choose."

"Faugh!" Jerry repeated.

"Sfaw!" said Hugh.

"Faugh - " Jerry began, but Dick interrupted.

"If you two asses are trying to say pshaw you are both wrong. I happened to see it in the dictionary a few days ago and it is pronounced shaw; it's a silly sort of word anyhow. No one uses it in real life. Shut your jaws and stop your shaws and let's go and get a drink."

"You can go," said Hugh, whose feelings were injured by the lack of interest in his new grape. "I'm going to stay here for the present."

"Leave him alone and he'll come home and bring his grape behind him," sang Grizzel, as they set off down the hill. Hugh pretended not to hear.

"I wish I was a Red Indian," he muttered to himself, as he watched the little party straggling down the road. "I'd invent some first-rate tortures for Grizzel."

The children trudged along the track between the trees. The air was full of dust stirred up by the carts, the sun seemed to grow hotter and hotter every moment, "putting on a sprint before the finish", Dick groaned, and the children grew thirstier and thirstier, till Mollie felt she could hardly bear it for one minute more. Her lips and tongue were dry and parched, and, although she kept her mouth shut, the dust blew up her nose and down her dry throat. She felt as if the sun were hitting her on the back between her shoulders, and her feet kept stumbling over the deep ruts in the road. "A Guide's motto is never say die till you are dead," she thought to herself. "There *are* times when I wish I were not a Guide, and this is one of them. 'Be Loyal.' Oh - *bother* Baden-Powell!" She held up three fingers to remind herself of the Guide Law, and tried her best to smile. "How do the others get on without it?" she wondered, watching Prue and Grizzel as they loitered along just before her, Grizzel dragging weary little feet in the dust. "I suppose they are used to it. Life in Australia isn't *all* beer and skittles. I wonder what skittles are? If they are something nice to drink I wish we had some here. Even beer would be better than nothing. I *am* a beautiful Patrol Leader! Walking behind and grousing for all I am worth." She hurried her steps a little and made up to the boys.

"Let's make a queen's chair and carry Grizzel," she suggested. "She looks about done. We can do it in turns, Dick and me, then Prue and Jerry."

"Righto!" said both boys at once.

"But you girls needn't do it," Dick added. "Jerry and I have carried heavier loads than that, haven't we, old son-of-a-gun?"

"Faugh!" said Jerry, with a wink.

Fortunately for the boys, and for Mollie, whose pride as a Patrol Leader was now up in arms, and perhaps most fortunately for Grizzel, whose weight was by no means fairy-like, they were overtaken at that moment by an empty cart, the driver of which pulled up and invited them all to jump in. It was a relief to sit down, though the floor of the cart was far from clean, and they were rattled and bumped like dried peas in a basket. Mollie thought the road would never end, and began to wonder at what stage of thirst delirium came on. But the longest lane has a turning, and at last they came in sight of a white house standing in the middle of an untidy sort of garden. The usual balcony ran round it, but this time it was approached by a wide flight of steps leading up from the drive in front. The cart stopped before a wooden gate, and without a word Prue led the way to the back veranda, where a row of canvas bags hung swinging from the roof. There were taps in the bags, but Prue ignored them. She climbed on to the veranda railing, dipped a tumbler into a bag, and handed it down to Mollie.

Oh, the exquisite joy of that drink! The water was deliciously cold; it trickled over Mollie's parched tongue, irrigated her dried-up throat, washed away the dust she had been inhaling, and in half a minute made her feel like a newly-made-over girl.

"It is worth while being thirsty," she said, as she watched the others revive under the same treatment. "I never knew before what a delicious thing water is. I'd like some more, please."

"I wish we were all giraffes," Grizzel said, with a sigh. "I'd like to have a throat a yard long and just sit here for ever letting cold water bubble down its hotness."

"What about Hugh?" asked Jerry, his conscience smiting him now that the irritating effect of heat and thirst had departed, and he reflected that his slighting remarks were probably the cause of Hugh's absence from this refreshing entertainment. "I expect he is the thirstiest of the lot, seeing he is the only one who did any work."

"He had his billy-can of cold tea with him this morning," Prue answered, "and if he *is* thirsty it is his own fault for being so huffy. Anyhow, he likes to practise enduring things; he says it is a useful habit. The worst of it is he thinks everyone else should endure too. I don't see the slightest use in making disagreeable things happen ten times just in case they should have to happen once."

Hugh seemed to have forgotten his grievance when he got home. He arrived along with Mr. von Greusen, who came to supper and talked to Papa about vintages and vines, the prospects of the wine industry, the possibilities of olive culture, and other subjects interesting to Australians but a trifle dull for the English listeners. Presently, however, the name of John Smith was introduced, and the boys pricked up their ears.

"He asks many questions," said Mr. von Greusen, "but I do not think that his heart is in the vineyard, as the heart of a man must be if he wishes to make his wine world-famous. In your work, that is where your heart must be, my children," he added, looking solemnly at the boys.

"And where do you think that the heart of Mr. John Smith is?" Papa asked, with a twinkle in his blue eyes.

"Ah!" said Mr. von Greusen, shaking his head, "that know I not. The heart of a young man who brings himself to Australia and whose feet tread the vineyard while his eyes look far away, so that he repeatedly trips over obstacles - where is it?" He shook his head again and hummed in a melodious baritone:

"Mädchen mit dem rothen Mündchen
Mit den Äuglein süss und klar."

"Aha!" laughed the professor, "I have seen more than one young man come to Australia to cure *that* disease. But I don't recommend the vineyard."

"I also not. Mr. John Smith should squat," said Mr. von Greusen.

Mollie laughed so suddenly that she choked, and brought a look of disapproval upon herself from her hostess.

"You may go, children. Mr. von Greusen wishes to hear you play, Prudence. Wait in the drawing-room till we come."

"Why did you go and laugh?" Hugh asked Mollie, as they trooped off to the drawing-room and thence to the balcony to enjoy the cool breeze which had sprung up. "I wanted to hear more about Mr. John Smith. I don't understand German. Do you? Why did Papa laugh?"

"I don't know much German, but I think *Mädchen* means girl," Mollie answered. "I couldn't help laughing. Squatting sounds such a funny cure for being in love." She giggled again.

"*Girl*!" Hugh exclaimed."*Girl*! I didn't think he was *that* sort of an idiot! He talked quite all right to me. No wonder Papa laughed. It's much funnier than squatting, I can tell you. There's nothing to laugh at in being a squatter. They're as rich as What's-his-name. Some of them are millionaires. I wish Papa was a squatter - but he would be no use on a sheep-run; you've got to be in the saddle all day, and keep your eyes skinned for blackfellows half the night. John Smith looked the very chap for it. *Girl*!"

"You needn't go on saying *girl* in that voice," said Grizzel. "It isn't the girl who is tumbling about with loverishness; it's Mr. Smith."

"What happened to the diamond-mine?" Mollie interrupted, feeling that another squabble was in the air. "Did you make a fortune, and is this house it?"

"Oh no - this house belongs to the Bertram Fitzherberts; they are fruit-farmers. They have gone home for a trip, and they told Papa to come here for the holidays, if he liked. Mr. von Greusen looks after the farm for them. His vineyard begins a little farther up the hill. The diamond-mine hasn't begun to pay yet, but it soon will."

"Do you like - is Mr. von Greusen a nice man?" Mollie asked hesitatingly; it felt a little queer to be such friends with the late (or the future, Mollie was a trifle mixed) enemy.

"Nice! Of course he is. Jolly nice, and jolly clever too. Why do you ask?"

"Oh - I don't know - he is a foreigner, and sometimes foreigners are - they're different."

"I don't know what you mean by different. Everybody is different from everybody else. Anyhow, he isn't a foreigner here; he is an Australian."

"What happens if you go to war?" asked Dick.

"We don't go to war. We are too far away to fight against other countries, and we will never fight each other, like America, and France, and the Wars of the Roses. There's nothing to fight about and there never will be. Of course - if we *wanted* to we *could*. We'd be first-class fighters if we weren't so peaceful. In fact," Hugh continued, in a somewhat dreamy tone, "I have invented, or at least thought about, several rather good things for fighting with - but they will never be wanted in Australia. Papa says that if ever there was a sweet and blessed country on earth it is Australia; it is full of peace and goodwill towards all men."

The English children were silent. It was a good thing, they thought, that people could not see into the future. Time-travelling was certainly best done backwards. And yet - who would want to wipe out the record of the Anzacs? Life was a fairly puzzling job, when you saw too far ahead.

"Papa says," Grizzel repeated, "that Australian people

Lydia Miller Middleton

ought to be the goodest people in the world, because there is a beautiful Cross always shining in the sky to remind us of the Beloved Son, like the rainbow, so that we should never forget. But I do. Nothing in the world seems to keep me from forgetting to be good just when I most want to remember." Grizzel heaved a sigh from the very bottom of her sinful little heart.

Everyone's eyes turned towards the Southern Cross, conspicuous even amongst the myriad stars shining and throbbing with tropical brilliance in the velvety blackness of the sky. Mollie remembered that it decorated the Australian flag, and she wondered if the sight of it had made the soldiers homesick sometimes. They were *real* Australians, she thought to herself, born and bred in this sunny land. She could remember a day when she had been walking with her mother in the Pimlico Road - a dark, foggy, raw day in late autumn. They had come upon a group of Australian soldiers standing round the door of a little green-grocer's shop, and chaffing the good-natured shop-woman about the quality of her fruit. Mother had stopped to speak to them. Mollie could not remember exactly what had passed, but the men had been friendly and communicative, and if they had groused about the English climate they had some cause, she thought, considering the climate they had come from; and they were cheerful about the war - she could remember that, for their voices had followed them through the fog singing "Australia will be there!" to what she had thought was a very lively and pleasant tune - and yet Mother had tears in her eyes. It was a good idea, she reflected, having that device on the flag, for it really was a bit of home - for them. Poor men! Suddenly a new thought came into her mind.

"Look!" she whispered, laying a hand on Jerry's arm and pointing to the Cross, "look! how brightly it shines! *Their name liveth for evermore!*"

Prue had slipped indoors and was playing a grave prelude and fugue of Bach's. The three older people joined the children in the balcony, and sat quietly listening till she had finished.

"That was very good, my child," said Mr. von Greusen, patting her approvingly on the shoulder, "very good indeed. Next winter we shall study together some piano and violin duets. And now perhaps your *verehrte Frau Mutter* will make some of her beautiful music for us. Some Schubert songs, yes?"

So Mamma went in, and she and Mr. von Greusen both made beautiful music, separately and together, which the audience in the balcony enjoyed without troubling to understand, Prue being the only one among them who loved music with her head as well as with her heart.

A sound of footsteps on the path below attracted the children's attention. Someone was walking slowly backwards and forwards, obviously listening to the music. As he passed through the long beam of light sent out by the lamp into the darkness, he turned up his face for a moment.

"It is Mr. John Smith," Hugh said in a low voice. "Shall I ask him to come up, Papa? He looks lonely out there all by himself."

"By all means ask him to come up," Papa whispered cordially; "but go quietly, my son, or Mamma will be out to know who is there, and our concert will be over."

Hugh departed on his errand, returning in a few moments with a tall figure in his wake, which he led to one of the long cane chairs scattered about, and left to its own meditations.

The children looked curiously at Mr. John Smith, He appeared to be a dark-haired young man, with a considerable amount of nose and chin and a good many inches of leg. He sat very still, his eyes fixed on the starry sky before him. There was, in his general outline in the semi-darkness of the balcony, something vaguely familiar to Mollie - one of those tantalizing impressions that come and go and refuse to be laid hold of.

"But I *can't* have seen him before," she said to herself; "it is quite impossible." She looked away and tried to get to where she had been before Mr. Smith came up - to that fairyland which the musician summons up with a wave of his magic wand, especially perhaps for those who love music mostly with their hearts, but the teasing little impression disturbed her like an imp. Until the notes of Schubert's "Adieu" came floating out into the night and carried them all on its wings up to the very gates of Heaven.

The sound of the piano closing brought them back to earth. The musicians stepped out on to the balcony.

"*Ende vom Lied,*" Mr. von Greusen said, as he left the lighted room behind him, "and the end of the evening too, for me. I must be getting home - hullo, Smith! Where did you come from? Am I to have the pleasure of introducing you to Professor and Mrs. Campbell, or has someone stolen a march upon me?"

"I brought him up," Hugh answered. "He heard Mamma singing and was fascinated like flies and moths and things."

They laughed as Mr. Smith made his apologies while he joined in the laughter. "You must come again," Mamma said, "and we will have a concert properly prepared for you. And you will give me all the news from home," she added, with the wistful note that was so often in her voice, "unless you will come in now, and try our Australian wine?"

But the young man could not stay, and, after a few more words of thanks and a grateful promise to come again at the earliest possible opportunity, he went off with Mr. von Greusen.

"Who *is* Mr. Smith?" Mollie asked, as they moved bedwards. "Doesn't anybody know who he is?"

"He is a young man newly out from home, and that is enough for Papa and Mamma," Hugh answered, with a yawn. "What does it matter who he is so long as he is a nice chap."

"But suppose he was a bushranger in disguise and -"

"Suppose he is Nebuchadnezzar, King of the Jews," Hugh interrupted, with another yawn. "I'm going to bed. We shall sleep tonight, with that cool wind. Thank goodness."

Next morning found them again on the winding road

which led up to the vineyards. For three-quarters of the way it ran through the woods of yesterday; then they left the woods behind and emerged on to a bare and shadeless track on the hill-side, and ten minutes later they turned in through the gate of the vineyard Mr. Von Greusen had given them permission to "browse" in, as he had expressed it. The English children had never seen a vineyard in their lives, and their expectations were inclined to be romantic and artistic. Large bunches of thin-skinned, bloomy purple grapes, hanging gracefully down from something like a pergola, was the picture they had formed in their minds. Mollie, it is true, had seen grapes growing in the cherry garden, but they had been so surrounded by cherry trees and other exciting objects that they had not left any great impression.

They found the reality somewhat disappointing. Here were acres of straight green lines hardly higher than gooseberry-bushes, and without a single tree to break the monotony or to cast a welcome shade. The bunches of grapes looked inviting enough, hanging among their decorative leaves and tendrils, but they had not been thinned and consequently were smaller than English hothouse grapes, while exposure to wind and dust had removed most of their bloom; but, in spite of their comparatively homely appearance, the children soon found that the fruit tasted sweet and luscious as only freshly gathered, sun-ripened fruit can do.

"This is Mr. von Greusen's experimental field," Hugh explained. "He mostly grows different lots for different wines, but here he has all sorts. We like these Ladies' Fingers; they go off in your mouth with such a nice squelch."

"What happens if you eat his favourite experiment?" asked Jerry, squelching his way diligently through a bunch of long, slender grapes of a translucent pale-green colour.

"He says, *'Donnerwetter*! What see I?'" Hugh answered; "but he ties a red worsted round his first-class experiments and then we know. He has tied *all* my new grapes up except the bunch he took home."

Now that the children were in the vineyard, and heard Hugh talking learnedly of Black Portugals, Verdeilho, Shirez, and other strange-sounding names, they were more reverential towards his new grape, which *might* be called Hughenne, or even, he generously suggested, either Gordello or Campdonne.

"It has to have a winey sound, you see," he said, "or it wouldn't sell. I think 'Gordello' sounds rather well myself."

It did not take very long to satisfy their appetite for grapes. The sun got hotter, their eyes ached with the glare, and they decided to return to the coolness of the woods and gardens lower down. The boys wanted to go exploring; the girls were to be left to collect peaches and melons for the new drink - which might bear the honoured name of Gordello until the famous champagne was put on the market - which would then be ready and cooling in the spring of the Fairy Dell by the time that the explorers were weary of exploring. Thus planned the boys.

"Boys propose, girls dispose," paraphrased Mollie, as the three pith helmets disappeared, after their owners had condescended to gather a share of the

Gordello-destined grapes and carry them part of the way towards the Dell. "If Dick and Jerry want drinks they can jolly well come and make them. *I* am going to have a rest."

Prue looked a little shocked, but Grizzel heartily agreed with Mollie. "I shall pull six peaches and one water-melon *exactly*," she said. "I am tired and my legs ache, and I can't be bothered with Hugh and his old Gordello."

A short walk down the road between the gum trees brought them to the fruit gardens, where Mollie saw peaches that made up by their magnificence for any hothouse elegance lacking in the grapes. Large as apples, soft and downy as velvet, glowing with crimson and gold, they were a perfect revelation of what peaches could be when they tried, and Mollie could hardly bear to wait till they reached the Fairy Dell before devouring one. But Prudence was firm.

"No, Mollie; not after all those grapes while you are hot and tired. Come and get your water-melon, and we'll go straight to the Dell and rest and eat peaches there. If you ate them now you might die all of a sudden, and that would be *so* awkward for Grizzel and me."

Mollie thought it would be more awkward for her, but did not argue. She followed Prue obediently, finding her basket of grapes, plus six peaches and a large water-melon, quite enough to absorb all her energies. If only Gordello were an accomplished fact, she thought, it would be very delightful. If someone else had made it and *she* could find it "cooling in the spring", as the boys expected to do, it would be extraordinarily delicious, and the more she thought of it the more delicious it became in her fancy. Poor boys! She was sorry for the disappointment awaiting them. Australians seemed to be a strenuous lot of people; no wonder the Australian soldiers were so brown and chinny.

Her meditations on chinny Australians lasted till they reached the Fairy Dell, the sight of which chased every other thought from her head. Surrounded by she-oaks and native cherry trees a smoothly curved hollow lay at the foot of a rocky declivity, its sides clothed with ferns almost startlingly green amidst the dried-up grass which covered most of the country around. A silvery cascade of water fell down the rock at the far side, its fine spray blown by the wind over the little hollow, looking in the sunlight like the veil of a fairy bride. Mollie recognized the delicate fronds of maidenhair growing in clumps here and there, and the edge of the pool at the bottom of the hollow was fringed with wild forget-me-nots.

The children scrambled down and seated themselves in a shady spot, untying their sun-bonnets and holding their hot and dusty faces towards the filmy veil of foam.

"It is heavenly," Mollie said, with a long sigh, as she sniffed up the cool scent of the damp ferns. "I don't wonder you call it the Fairy Dell."

"It is Mamma's favourite spot, and we often have picnics here," said Prue, hanging her sun-bonnet on a branch of she-oak that spread above them. "There's the water all ready, you see, and there's a place up there where we can light our fire. Mamma sketches, and we bring our books or we hunt for wild flowers; it is always a nice place to be in. Now we can eat our fruit." She produced a knife from her basket and cut a melon in halves. Its delicate pink flesh and black seeds called forth more enthusiastic admiration from Mollie.

"Let us arrange all the things among the ferns," she suggested, "and gather some forget-me-nots to put beside that pink melon; then the purple grapes; then the peaches - isn't it *pretty*, Prue?"

Prue nodded her head; she was speechless with melon, and soon the other two were following her example; and melon was followed by peaches.

Then Grizzel jumped to her feet. "There is a cache here," she said. "Papa often pops something in for a surprise when he passes this way. I'm going to look; there might be a pencil there, and I want to draw that fruit."

She soon returned, carrying in her hand a small basket, which yielded up two books, a small sketching-block, and a box of chocolates. "You can have the books," she announced, "one is *From Six to Sixteen*, by Mrs. Ewing, and the other is *Twenty Thousand Leagues under the Sea*, by Jules Verne."

Mollie, being the guest, got first choice and took Jules Verne, turning the pictures over with much interest as she compared the *Nautilus* with the submarine of 1920.

"I do think," she said emphatically, helping herself to a large chocolate-cream with entire disregard of both past and future, "I do think that your father is a perfect *peach*."

Grizzel glanced up from her drawing to the still-life study before her. "He is more the shape of a water-melon," she remarked.

Mollie laughed.

"Be quiet, Grizzel," Prue said angrily. "How can you speak so disrespectfully of Papa? You should be ashamed of yourself."

"I'm *not* disrespectful," Grizzel answered indignantly. "I think it is a beautiful shape."

Mollie laughed again.

"You *are* disrespectful," Prue repeated, turning very red. "Papa does the dearest, sweetest things, and all your thanks is to make Mollie laugh at him. It is horrible of you, and I don't call it very nice of Mollie."

"I'm not laughing at your father," Mollie said; "I wouldn't dream of doing such a thing. I'm laughing at Grizzel. She is so funny."

"I'm *not* funny," said Grizzel, turning as red as Prudence, "and if you laugh at Papa for being partly the shape of a water-melon, I'll laugh at *your* father. Your father is an unripe olive and your mother is a bitter almond," she added vindictively.

But if she expected Mollie to be insulted she was disappointed, for that young person went off into fits of cackling giggles which she vainly tried to suppress. At last she rose to her feet.

"I've got the giggles badly," she spluttered out. "I get

them sometimes. I think I had better go away for a little till I am better. I *really* am not laughing at your father. I think he is a perfectly lovely father."

"Then you shouldn't call names," said Prue, still very red. "How would you like me to call your father an apricot?"

"I shouldn't mind in the least," answered Mollie, giggling worse than ever. "You don't understand. I'll go away, and I'll explain when I am better."

She seized her sunbonnet, tucked her book under her arm, climbed up the side of the ferny dell, crossed the track, and ran into the wood on the farther side, leaving Prue and Grizzel to finish the squabble between themselves.

"We have eaten too much, that's what's the matter," she said to herself, as she slowed down to a walk and the giggle became less severe. "This hot sun all the time makes one feel crossish."

She came to a halt at the foot of a hollow gum tree, and stooping a little she peered within. It looked shady and cool, its floor powdered with decayed bark mixed with dead leaves - quite clean enough, she decided, to sit upon and rest until her giggles had finally subsided. She crept in, snuggled down comfortably, opened her book, and soon was deep in the adventures of Professor Arrownax, Ned Land, Captain Nemo, and the rest.

The shadows swung slowly round, the sun climbed higher and higher, and the day grew hotter and hotter, but Mollie, skimming along the bottom of the sea in the *Nautilus* was oblivious of heat. She was walking in the submarine forest of the Island of Crespo, treading on sand "sown with the impalpable dust of shells", when the sudden cracking of a sun-dried branch near at hand startled her and reminded her that time was passing. She closed her book, crept out of her tree, and set off towards the Dell.

"I wish," she said impatiently to herself, "that Time would find something new to do. His one idea seems to be to pass. He may fly or he may crawl, but he is *incessantly* passing."

She stood still as she spoke and looked before her. Surely the trees were growing more closely together than they had seemed to do; their tall grey-white trunks repeated themselves in a most bewildering way, and right in her path lay a fallen giant which she was perfectly certain she had not passed before.

"Bother! I have come the wrong way," she said, turning round and retracing her steps. "I remember now, there were some trees with rings cut round their trunks - there they are."

She reached the ringed trees, turned her back upon them, and walked straight on. But she came to a dried-up creek which she had not seen before. She could not have missed seeing it, for it was too wide to jump. And there were more ringed trees.

"I can't be far from the Dell, that's one thing certain. I'll coo-ee."

She coo-eed her best and shrillest, but no answer came. There was no sound but the occasional scamper of some small furry animal or the unhomely call of an Australian parrot or magpie. All around her the monotonous grey trunks stood, as much alike as the pillars of a town-hall, and overhead the blue-green leaves stirred languidly in the warm wind. Mollie was standing, though she did not know it, on primeval forest land.

What she did begin to realize was that she was lost.

"I *can't* be far away," she repeated to herself. "I wasn't running for five minutes. The point is, how am I to find the way back. Everything is so difficult in this upside-down place; I haven't the least idea which is north and which is south; nor which way the wind blows, nor how the shadows fall, nor *anything*; and if I go the wrong way I will only get farther and farther from the Dell. The best plan really is to sit down and wait till someone comes. Someone is sure to look for me sooner or later; Dick and Jerry will, anyhow." She looked about her again in search of inspiration. Sitting down and waiting was not a cheerful prospect. Dick and Jerry might whisk away home and leave her behind. Or she might merely wake up suddenly and find herself in the Chauncery morning-room, safe but dull, or - just supposing she didn't! Supposing that she couldn't get back without Prue, and that she turned into an interesting case for the What's-its-name Society, to be read about in learned books!

"I might try climbing a tree," she thought, gazing round in search of something climbable. But the tall, smooth trunks were discouraging; there were few with boughs within her reach, and the few there were were too low to be of any use as observation posts. She sat down and resolutely opened her book. "Never say die till you are dead," she repeated, firmly fastening the Guide's smile on to her face. "I'll read, and coo-ee every third page."

But she no longer walked in the submarine forest; she only sat in a wood and read about other people doing it, lifting her eyes from the page every now and then, and turning her head uneasily from side to side, feeling very lonely in that great, still place!

What was that? A magpie or a human whistle? " - two-three, *one*-two-three, *one* -". Someone was whistling the air from *Faust*. Mollie sprang to her feet and coo-eed with all her might and main. The whistling stopped short, and there was an answering shout in a man's voice. Mollie coo-eed again.

"Hi! You'll have to come to me," the man shouted; "I can't come to you. Tied here by the leg."

It is not an easy thing to locate a sound in the open air, and though Mollie had had some practice in the course of her Guide work, it was only after several shouts on the man's part and experiments on hers that she at last found herself standing beside Mr. John Smith, who was sitting on the ground with one bootless leg stretched out before him.

"I am glad to see you," he said to Mollie. "I have sprained my ankle rather badly, and was just wondering what to do next. There seemed to be nothing for it but to crawl all the way home, and the prospect was not pleasing."

"I am glad to see you too," said Mollie. "I am lost."

"Lost!" exclaimed the young man. "Oh no, you aren't. I have a compass, and it is not more than a couple of miles or so to Silver Fields, von Greusen's place. I'll show you how to use a compass, and you will be my good angel and go to Silver Fields and ask them to send a horse along, and I will be grateful to you for ever."

"I know how to use a compass, thank you," said Mollie, feeling greatly relieved, "and I will go to Mr. von Greusen's place if you tell me where it is; but first I will bandage up your foot and make it feel easier. I have learnt First Aid. May I take that thing off your hat for a bandage?" - as she noticed the pith helmet and pugaree lying on the ground.

"My pugaree? Good idea! I don't know what First Aid is precisely, but it sounds appropriate. Do you mean you can fix a bandage?"

"Rather," said Mollie, comfortably conscious that she was a First-class Guide and a bright and shining light in this particular line. "How did you sprain your ankle? I suppose you -" she stopped short. She had almost said that she supposed he had tripped over an obstacle in a fit of loverishness. "I suppose your foot just went. That's what mine did."

"I caught it in a rabbit-hole," he answered, "the floor of Australia seems to be perforated with them. Why didn't you coo-ee sooner?"

"I did," Mollie answered, as she unwound the pugaree and took off her patient's sock, " I coo-eed ever so often - oh, dear me! that *is* a bad foot! I'm afraid you'll be laid up for ever so long. Why didn't *you* coo-ee?"

"I did," answered Mr. Smith, eyeing the badly swollen and discoloured ankle ruefully. "I coo-eed ever so often too. I suppose we mistook each other for magpies. Next time I'll try a good English shout. Now, what's to happen? D'ye mean to say that I'm to be stuck up in Silver Fields for goodness knows how long with only my own thoughts for company and nothing to do? Oh, ye gods and little fishes!" he groaned disconsolately.

"I'm afraid so," Mollie replied sympathetically. "I sprained my ankle -" she was going to say "the other day" but remembered in time - "once in the holidays, and I had to lie on a sofa all day. It wasn't nearly so dull as I expected though," she ended with a little laugh. As they talked she had been skilfully bandaging the swollen ankle in her best style, which was a style not to be despised by anybody. "Now," she said, as she tucked in the end and fastened it firmly with her Tenderfoot brooch, "now you will be more comfortable. But you must keep quite still. I do wish you were not so far from home; you should not ride. If you do anything foolish now you may be lame all your life; that's what the doctor told me; he was most frightfully firm about it. Your wrist is bleeding - you have cut it."

The young man turned back his shirt sleeve. "It is nothing. A handkerchief twisted round will do. You have done the bandage beautifully."

Mollie arranged the handkerchief. As she did so her eyes fell upon a tattoo-mark, an anchor inside a true-lover's knot. It was an ordinary enough tattoo-mark, but the sight of it struck at Mollie for *she had seen it before*. The odd impression of last night, which she had forgotten in the various exigences of the situation, came rushing back into her mind. Who *did* he remind her of? How could she possibly have seen that little mark before?

"My name is John Smith," he said, looking up and finding her eyes fixed questioningly upon him. "I don't think we have met before?"

"I saw you last night at the Campbell's," Mollie replied aloud (while to herself she added, "And where I saw you before that is what I should like to know more than anything else at this present moment"). "I am staying there. It was dark on the balcony and there were a lot of us children; you wouldn't notice me. My name is Mollie - oh, you simply must *not* twist your leg about like that! Your ankle *may* be broken; you don't know."

He smiled; his eyes crinkled up and there was a something in the tilt of his mouth. Why was that smile so familiar? Was it the Prince of Wales? No, it was someone she knew much better than she knew the Prince of Wales. (Which wasn't saying very much after all.)

"You are very cheery! So you were there, were you? I never heard such heavenly singing in my life. Von Greusen says that Mrs. Campbell has one of the most beautiful voices in South Australia, and I should say that he has the other. But it isn't only their voices, it's the way they sing, making you think of all the might-have-beens and ought-to-have-beens and never-will-bes -" he stopped, and sighed in a melancholy way, leaning his back against the tree behind him. "I think you had better be starting, Miss Polly. Neither of us will be the worse of getting home."

"Mollie, not Polly. I wish you had not to be left alone. I will be as quick as I can. How shall I describe this place? I think I had better come back with the men."

"No need for that. Tell them I'm by the creek on the way to the olive plantation. They'll know. I have a sister called Polly. I was thinking of her at that moment," he added, with another sigh. "I had a letter from her yesterday and she wants me to go back. The point is, shall I go or shall I not?"

"I don't know, but I think I had better hurry," Mollie said. It had occurred to her that if *she* "went back" with her usual abruptness, before she delivered her message, Mr. John Smith might be left in an awkward predicament.

He handed over the compass with careful directions. She nodded her head, waved her hand at her distractingly perplexing new acquaintance, and set off. Soon her entire attention was absorbed in finding her way, for, although she had used a compass often enough when Guiding, an Australian forest was something quite new, and to her it seemed as trackless as the ocean, every part of it looked so precisely the same as every other part. Eventually, however, she found herself safely back on the cart-track, though nowhere within sight of the Fairy Dell. She decided to go straight home to the Campbell's house and ask there for help for Mr. John Smith. Mr. Von Greusen would probably be out at this hour, and she felt shy of the big bearded men working about the place.

Mamma was in, and heard her story with concern.

"Of course he must come here," she exclaimed, with

true Australian hospitality, unquestioning and ungrudging. "He must be properly nursed and fed." Mollie thought that Mamma looked rather pleased than otherwise at the prospect of nursing and feeding a good-looking young man newly out from home. Bridget was called, and between them all a room was got ready and made to look as homelike as possible. "Flowers and books," said Mrs. Campbell, "always make a room look pleasant. I wish I had some photographs. I wonder who his people are. We'll put up a picture of St. Paul's Cathedral, and this little water-colour of a Sussex village; they are not quite the same thing as his mother or sweetheart, but they will be better than nothing." She sighed as she looked at the water-colour. They were great people for sighing, Mollie thought. It must be rather miserable to be homesick so very, very far away from home!

When Prudence and Grizzel, accompanied by the boys, all not a little anxious about Mollie, arrived at home for dinner they found not only the missing Mollie but also Mr. John Smith on the balcony. Mollie ran down the steps to meet them, and gave a highly coloured account of her adventures. Past differences were forgiven and forgotten, and after dinner they all assembled on the balcony again with the benevolent intention of devoting themselves to the entertainment of the interesting invalid.

But Mrs. Campbell did not approve of this plan. "We are too many," she said in her decided way. "Prudence and Mollie may stay; the rest of you must run away for the present. Grizzel can go for a walk with Bridget and Baby; I want a few things from the Store, and they can be brought up in the perambulator. The boys had better go up to Mr. von Greusen's and see about getting Mr.

Smith's belongings brought here."

"You might call at the Fairy Dell and get the Gordello," Prudence suggested - for after all she and Grizzel had made the new drink in a fit of remorse - "Mr. Smith will perhaps like to taste it."

The family melted away, and Mamma with the two girls settled down to needlework. Mamma's kindly interest invited confidence under these pleasant circumstances, and it was not long before the young man was pouring his story into her sympathetic ears. Prudence listened spellbound. It was not often that one had romance brought to one's very door - by a hero with a sprained ankle too! Such a romantic affliction! But Mollie was too much preoccupied by that haunting likeness to listen properly to what the hero was saying, once she had ascertained the fact that Mr. Smith belonged to the Campbell's Time, and that therefore she could not possibly have met himself before; it must have been somebody extraordinarily like him. And yet - the number of her friends was not so very great that one could be totally forgotten. She tried not to think about it, but it stuck in the back of her brain in an irritating sort of way and refused to be forgotten.

His story was not at all an uncommon one: a love-affair, a selection of angry parents, lack of money, eternal vows, and a young man in search of a fortune. He had been told that fortunes lay about loose in Australia.

"Not that I mind working," he said. "I like work all right, but it's so slow, and we are getting older all the time. I rather fancied a vineyard; our parents are great on their cellars and might come round to a vineyard and wine. I spent some time in France before coming here, but it was hopeless. They won't look at a foreigner in their wine concerns. As a matter of fact I have some hopes of my own governor relenting. I am his only son, and he is getting tired of keeping me at arm's length. There's nothing really in the way; only he had another wife in view for me, and Margaret's father had another husband. *He* is rather a cantankerous old party. Too much port wine is what is the matter with them both, that's my opinion; they're turning gouty."

As Mr. John Smith talked he pulled his watch out of his pocket and sprung it open. In the back lay a tiny photograph.

"That's Margaret," he said.

The others bent over the faintly tinted portrait of a young girl, pretty and smiling, her wavy hair rippling on either side of a smooth brow. Mollie glanced at it absent-mindedly; the back of her brain, she felt, was moving to the front; in another moment it would be there.

Mr. Smith looked affectionately at the pretty face. "That is my little girl," he repeated, "and I - I ought to tell you - you are so kind - my name is not really John Smith. I dropped my real name because I wanted to dodge my governor - teach him a lesson, you know, not to play fast and loose with his only son - poor old governor! I have written to him since I came to Silver Fields. My real name is -

Suddenly Mollie began to laugh. It had come in a flash - the long chair, the bandaged foot on a foot-rest, the watch with its back open, the tattooed anchor and rope on a lean wrist, and above all a pair of dark eyes (so like Dick's) crinkled up in a kindly smile: "You don't blow hard enough, little Polly," someone was saying, "try again." The hair above the dark eyes was white, but Mollie knew.

"It's so *funny*," she cried, as they all looked at her, Prudence anxiously inquiring if she had "got it again". "I'm all right, Prue, but it's so funny. *I* know who you are," she laughed again, turning to Mr. Smith. "Your name isn't John Smith at all. You are poor dear Richard. Who was so active. With the gout. And you are - you are my -"

"Hush, Mollie!" said Prue.

* * * * *

Mollie sat up. She was still laughing. Aunt Mary stood beside her in hat and coat, her hands full of cardboard boxes from Buszard's. Grannie sat at the tea-table, and opposite her was old Mrs. Pell, who had put on her bonnet because it would soon be time for her to go. They all looked at Mollie, who continued to laugh.

"It's nothing," she said. "It is only a fit of giggles. I have them sometimes."

"Give the dear child her tea, Mary," said Grannie. "Her nerves are a little highly strung; her grandfather used to laugh just like that - poor dear Richard!"

CHAPTER VII

The Aeronauts or The Fateful Stone

"Aunt Mary, how old is Time?" asked Mollie.

She was resting on her sofa in the garden, after her first attempt at a short walk. She had been wondering how her young grandpapa had got on with his sprained ankle, and longed to ask questions about him, but dared not venture even on the simplest. It was so easy to forget and ask too much. The day was rather hot, and the couch had been drawn into the shade of a great copper-beech. Mollie lay on her back, gazing up through the silky red foliage at the blue sky. Somewhere a thrush was singing, practising his flute-like phrases with conscientious care.

"I think he must be trying for a scholarship," said Mollie. "How old is Time?" she repeated, bringing her gaze down from the tree-tops to Aunt Mary's hands, busy as usual with needlework.

"How old is Time?" Aunt Mary echoed. "What do you mean exactly by Time?"

"I mean, how long is it since days began - morning and afternoon and evening?"

"Untold millions of years," her aunt answered. "I don't suppose that anyone could say exactly how many, and in any case when we speak of Time we mean Time on our own earth; what an astronomer would say I don't know."

"How do you know that it is millions of years old?" Mollie asked. "In the Bible it says that the evening and the morning were the first day in the year 4004 B.C. That is only five thousand, nine hundred and twenty-four years ago."

"You are asking terribly big questions," Aunt Mary said, with a smile. "It would take a long time to explain how men learnt to know the age of the world, and I am afraid I am hardly equal to the task. It is only about seventy years since geologists began to suspect that our earth was far older than they had supposed, I have some simple books which I think you could understand if you tried; and if you learn to take an interest in geology you need never be dull again as long as you live. You will find 'tongues in trees, books in the running brooks, sermons in stones, and good in everything'."

"That would be very nice," Mollie said politely but not enthusiastically; "but just now I only want to know how old Time is. Millions and millions of years," she repeated to herself rather dreamily. "If you took forty from millions and millions it wouldn't make any difference worth mentioning. It makes even Adam seem almost as near as last week. And this morning I said I hadn't time to darn a hole in my stocking. I wonder if Eve said she had no time. Were there any people before Adam, Aunt Mary?"

Aunt Mary shook her head. "Ask the wise thrush," she said; "his ancestors are older than mine."

"Are they really!" Mollie exclaimed. "Did that thrush's ever-so-great-grandfather sing in the Garden of Eden?"

Aunt Mary only answered with a smile, and Mollie listened again to the thrush, her thoughts wandering back to the times of forty years ago. Quite a little time, she mused. No wonder they were so little different, considering all things, from our own. She had thought that the children of those days must be frightfully dull, and terribly strictly kept; but on the whole they were, in some ways, less dull - or more exciting - and certainly had more liberty, than the children of to-day. Perhaps, however, that was Australia, where there was so much more room than there was in England. She wondered how Dick and Jerry were getting on to-day, and wished for the hundredth time that she could see them and talk things over. They had each other to talk to, but she had no one.

"Have you any diamonds, Aunt Mary?" she asked presently. "I should like to see some diamonds; and rubies and emeralds and topazes and opals and pearls and amethysts and sapphires, and all the precious stones you've got."

"Bless my soul, Mollie! Do you think I am the Queen of Sheba!" Aunt Mary exclaimed. "Grannie has some old-fashioned jewellery locked away in a drawer, but the family diamonds are nothing to go to law about. The only diamond I possess," she went on, "is a green diamond in a ring that someone gave me long, long ago. Long ago," she repeated with a sigh, letting her work drop into her lap and gazing at something that

The Happy Adventurers

Mollie could not see, for it was the distant past.

Mollie gave a violent start. A green diamond! In a ring! Long, long ago. How very extraordinary! She dared not ask any questions, but she examined her aunt with new and critical interest, from the shining coils of smooth brown hair to the slim ankles and neat buckled shoes. No, she decided, that hair could never have been red and ringletty; besides, Grizzel's eyes were blue and round like a kitten's, while Aunt Mary's were dark brown and long-shaped. Very pretty eyes, Mollie suddenly discovered. Also, Aunt Mary was too young. Forty years ago Grizzel was eight or nine years old, which would make her nearly fifty now. Mollie paused for a moment to picture to herself a fifty-year-old Grizzel, but, failing utterly in the attempt, she continued her meditations on her aunt. Aunt Mary was certainly a considerable distance from that venerable age. Mollie wondered again why she had never married, and who had given her that ring. She sighed impatiently. She wished that she was not bound down by that promise; but she was, hard and fast. It would be better not to think about the green diamond just now. When she got back to forty years ago she would keep her eyes open; it was not at all unlikely, considering all things, that Aunt Mary had had an Australian lover, and it might be possible to do a kind act somehow or other. What the effect would be if 1920 meddled about with the affairs of 1880 Mollie had ceased worrying over. It was altogether too puzzling.

Aunt Mary remained a little absent-minded all the morning, and when the time came for Mollie to go to sleep that afternoon she could hear a new tone in Aunt Mary's voice when she began to sing:

"O bay of Dublin! my heart you're troublin',
Your beauty haunts me like a fevered dream,
Like frozen fountains that the sun sets bubblin
My heart's blood warms when I but hear your name;
And never till this life pulse ceases,
My earliest thought you'll cease to be;
Oh! there's no one here knows how fair that
place is,
And no one cares how dear it is to me!"

"If Aunt Mary goes on like this, Prue will certainly find me howling my eyes out," Mollie said to herself. "Talk of might-have-beens and never-will-bes! Grandpapa should hear his own daughter singing! Why did I go and mention green diamonds to her!" She shut her eyes tight to keep the tears from falling. The plaintive tune went on, and when a small soft hand crept into her own her cheeks were wet. She kept her eyes closed and held tight to the little hand!

* * * * *

She was standing in a wide, brick-floored veranda with a steeply sloping roof. The open sides were wreathed with morning-glories, their deep-blue petals wide-spreading to the early sun. Painted tubs, full of scarlet and purple fuchsias, stood in a row beside the railing; coco-nut matting, rough and brown, lay in strips across the red brick floor, and at either end of the veranda stood a deal table. One was covered with books, toys, and work-baskets. At the other sat Bridget, shelling peas. She was singing:

"How often when at work I'm sittin',
An' musin' sadly on the days of yore,
I think I see my Katey knittin',

An' the children playin' by the cabin door;
I think I see the neighbours' faces
All gathered round, their long-lost friend to see,
Oh! though no one here knows how fair that
place is,
Heaven knows how dear my poor home was to me."

As she sang the last word she lifted the corner of her apron to dry her eyes, and saw Mollie.

"Is it yourself, Miss Mollie, or is it your ghost? May the Lord look sideways on me ould plaid shawl! You gave me a start then, for 'twas only this minute I looked to see an' there was no one there at all."

"It's me," said Mollie, swallowing down a few last tears and wondering if she was speaking the truth - perhaps it *was* her ghost! "Where's everybody?"

"They're all dressin' themselves for the balloonin', an' may the Lord preserve Master Hugh an' keep his bones from breakin'. 'Tis a temptin' o' Providence an' his mother sailin' on the salt seas, poor soul. The way the death-watch has been tickin' on me this wake past is something cruel."

"What's the ballooning?" Mollie began, but before Bridget could answer Prudence appeared at the house door, dressed in festive pink muslin and a white hat wreathed with rosebuds.

"Come along, Mollie," she said, "and don't listen to Bridget croaking. If I died every time she hears my death-watch tick, or sees my shroud in a candle, there would be a whole cemetery full of my graves by this time. There's a yellow muslin frock for you."

They had reached the girls' bedroom, which Mollie recognized as the first of the rooms she had slept in. They were back in the house with Hugh's tree and the yellow-carpeted garden. She looked admiringly at the pretty muslin frock on the bed. It was white, powdered over with tiny dots of pale yellow, and made with filmy flounces reaching to the waist; a frilled fichu, or "cross-over" as Prue called it, came over the front of the little bodice, falling slightly below the waist and tied behind with pale-yellow ribbons. A wide white hat was wreathed with primroses and green leaves. It was indeed a charming frock, and so modern that Mollie thought she might have worn it at home without anyone being surprised at anything except her unusual smartness. Prudence and Grizzel wore dresses fashioned in precisely the same way, but Prue's muslin was sprigged with pink rosebuds, while Grizzel's dots were green.

"Come along, my rainbow," said Papa. "If we are late we won't get a good place."

They walked down the cypress-bordered path of Mollie's first visit, and joined the stream of people going along the road, like themselves, to see the balloon ascent. Mollie felt very gay and festive; everybody feminine wore light frocks, the sun was bright but not too hot, the grass was green, and the whole countryside was frothed with almond-blossom, white and pink. Birds flew briskly about, indifferent to balloons, and horses with shining chestnut coats trotted along the well-kept road, lifting their slim ankles and polished heels in an elegant way very different from the gait of London cab-horses.

A balloon ascent was always a thrilling sight, Prudence

explained, but the particular thrill about this one was that Hugh was going up. The aeronaut was a friend of Papa's, and, Mamma being on her way home to England, it had not been difficult to persuade easy-going Papa to give his consent. Indeed, there was nothing that he would have liked better than to go up himself, but Mr. Ferguson had shaken his head over fifteen stone of useless passenger.

"If we could throw you out a pound at a time you would be most welcome," he had said; "but you must wait a bit, Professor; the day will come when we shall not have to count every pound."

When they reached the field they found a deeply interested crowd already collected, and Papa had some difficulty in getting his rainbow into a good position. The huge balloon towered up far above them, its striped smoke-coloured sides gleaming under the netted mesh as it swayed with every breath of wind. The wicker car looked very small and frail.

"It's not so small as it looks," Prue said to Mollie. "We were in it yesterday. It is nearly as big as my bedroom, and the sides reach up to Hugh's shoulder; he couldn't fall out unless he did it on purpose. There are dear little cubby-holes and all sorts of cute fixings. Its name is the *Kangaroo*. I do wish I could go up too, but Papa and Mr. Ferguson simply wouldn't hear of it. Girls are never allowed to do anything."

"Aren't you nervous?" Mollie asked. "Suppose it suddenly burst when it was ever so high. How high does it go?"

"Mr. Ferguson has been up five miles, but he is only

Lydia Miller Middleton

going up one to-day. They won't be very long away."

"You would be just as badly smashed if you fell one mile as if you fell five, I should think," said Mollie, with a shudder.

"It isn't falling that they think about," Prue explained, "When you get very high you can't breathe, and you have all sorts of horrid feelings. Once Mr. Ferguson fainted, and if the man with him hadn't pulled the stopper thing out with his teeth they'd both have been killed."

"Why teeth?" asked Mollie.

"Because his hands were frozen, and he couldn't use them," answered Prue. "They'll be starting soon; they are going on board - look, there's Hugh!"

Mollie saw a small grey-clad figure climbing into the car. He was followed by two men, one tall and the other rather short. As they climbed over the rails the great balloon swayed and trembled - it looked far more dangerous than a nice substantial aeroplane, Mollie thought; and there was no control, they simply flew up and were blown hither and thither according to the will of the winds. Suppose they were blown against something and got a great rip in the side!

"I don't know how you *can*," she said to Prue. "If it were Dick - where are Dick and Jerry? Haven't they come?"

"Here we are, old bean, at your elbow. My word, wouldn't I like to be going up too!"

"Same here. Some chaps have all the luck!" groaned Jerry.

Prudence shook her head. "Mr. Ferguson would never take more than one boy. Two might begin larking, and you simply must not lark in a balloon."

Dick thought of a joke about larks and balloons, but decided that it was not a really first-class joke and merely shook an accusatory head at boys and their reprehensible ways.

The ring of men who held down the balloon were preparing to let go the ropes; the band began to play, the men in the balloon took off their caps and waved farewell, people cheered - and the *Kangaroo* was off. She rose swiftly and buoyantly, remaining almost perpendicular until she was caught by a southwest current of air and sailed away towards the hills. As she rose the children could see Hugh at the edge of the car, waving his handkerchief.

It was very exciting. They stood and watched the *Kangaroo* for some time, but her progress was slow, and Papa remarked that they could see her just as well from the street as from the field, now that she was near the clouds. He looked at his watch:

"There is just time to go and have some lunch before your dinner. What would you say to cocoa and cream-cakes at Bauermann's?"

This suggestion cheered away the left-behindish feeling that they all experienced as they watched that distant pear-shaped object floating in the sky. As they walked along the road it was impossible to keep their eyes and thoughts from following the balloon, so that conversation was desultory, until Mollie thought she saw a bad wobble and gave a little scream.

"You really need not be so nervous," Prue said, catching her by the arm. "Mr. Ferguson has been up hundreds of times, he won't let Hugh down. Bridget read Hugh's fortune in his tea-cup last night and says he is going to die when he is eighty-three-and-a-half; I can't think why she has begun to hear his death-watch tick already. And besides - don't you believe in Fate? If it is your fate to fall from a balloon and be killed, you'll be killed that way; there's no use trying not to be."

"You couldn't be if you never went up in a balloon," said Mollie.

"Then it wouldn't be your fate," Prudence answered.

Mollie could not think of a suitable reply at the moment and was silent.

"That's not all," Grizzel added. "Hugh has got my green diamond with him for luck. Bridget says that my diamond is the Luck of the Campbells, and will always bring good luck to the person that wears it, like a four-leaved shamrock. So I made Hugh take it."

This remark reminded the others of the diamond-mine, and Dick, Jerry, and Mollie became eager for news of that adventure. It had turned out fairly well; they had not as yet made a fortune, but on the strength of their prospects Mr. Fraser had encouraged Papa to send Mamma and Baby for a trip home, and to add several comforts to the household, one of which was the broad veranda at the back of the house, in which Mollie had found herself that morning.

"We live in it by day, and some of us sleep in it by night," Prue said. "You shall sleep in a hammock to-night, Mollie."

After a feast of cocoa and cream-cakes at Bauermann's they got home just in time for a dinner of twice-laid and Uncle Tom's pudding, to which even Dick and Jerry could not do justice.

"It's my favourite dinner, too," sighed Prudence. "It's a strange thing that one day you get too much and another day too little. To-morrow there will be no Bauermann's and most likely dinner will be boiled mutton and tapioca pudding."

The afternoon passed rather slowly. Hugh might be back about five o'clock, and they were too anxious to hear how he had got on to be able to settle down to any occupation. They played croquet until all their tempers were hopelessly lost, even Prudence accusing Mollie of cheating. As if a Guide ever cheated under any circumstances whatsoever! After each girl in turn had thrown down her mallet and declared that she wouldn't play, Dick swiftly defeated Jerry, the party recovered its tempers, and they were sitting down to play "I met a One-horned Lady always Genteel" when the garden-gate clicked and Hugh appeared.

Now Dick and Jerry, each in his own mind, had suspected that Hugh would come back from his trip full of "swank", and each had decided that gently and politely, but very firmly, he would squash the swanker. But there was no sign of the conquering hero about

Hugh. He came slowly up the garden path towards them, gloom and depression showing in every step that he took, and still more upon his face as he drew near.

They looked at him expectantly, but he stood silently beside them, his shoulders stooping as though a load of care sat upon them, his usually clear eyes heavy and clouded, and the corners of his mouth turned down as if he had made up his mind never to smile again.

"What's up?" asked Jerry at last. "Did the balloon bust, and you the sole survivor?"

"Didn't my diamond bring you luck after all?" Grizzel questioned anxiously.

"Sick, old bean?" inquired Dick sympathetically.

"I think you'd better have tea right away," Prudence said, laying a motherly little hand on her brother's arm.

"If he's got something bad to tell he'd better tell it," said Mollie. "Nothing cures care like giving it air."

Hugh threw himself on the grass, hugged his legs with his arms, and, resting his chin on his knees, stared before him in stony silence.

"Spit it out, old bus," Dick adjured him, "If you are in a scrape we are with you to a man - aren't we?" he asked the others.

A chorus of agreement brought a flicker of light into the gloom of Hugh's face.

"I have been the biggest ass in the world," he said. "If

there is a bigger it would comfort me to meet him."

Two brown hands were promptly outstretched, but Hugh shook his head: "Wait till you hear." He paused for a moment, looked nervously from side to side and then behind him:

"I'm a murderer. Probably I shall be hanged. Unless I poison myself first."

"Hugh!" Prudence exclaimed sharply, "don't make these horrible jokes. You know how Mamma hates them."

"It isn't a joke, worse luck," Hugh groaned; "it's beastly true. Thank goodness Mamma is out of the way. Perhaps it can be hushed up so that she will never know the truth about the way I died."

A look of consternation settled upon every face; whatever Hugh had done, it was plain that he was exceedingly unhappy.

"Tell us," Jerry commanded briefly.

Hugh sat up. "I may as well," he agreed dejectedly. "You'd better hear it from me than from some old policeman. I suppose one will be stalking up the path soon." He was silent again for a minute, and then started once more:

"It was this way. When we went up first it was perfectly glorious - you never can imagine how lovely Adelaide looks from the air, with the hills round and the sea in the distance and almond-blossom all over the place. Oh - if only this thing hadn't happened I could tell you all sorts of things, but now I can't think of anything. It was near the end. I was awfully keen on trying an experiment - two experiments in fact. I wanted to see how near I could hit a given spot if I aimed at it with a stone, and I wanted to see how much the stone would deflect in falling. Perhaps it's only one experiment really, but it struck me as being two at the time. You see, if Australia ever goes to war we might want to shoot from balloons, or one might drop a ball of explosives with a fuse attached or something. I thought about it when that Russian scare was on, but I never thought I'd get the chance to try. So I got a good, smooth, round stone, nine-and-a-half ounces, and wrapped it up in a handkerchief and took it up. I knew a good place to aim at - the tree in Mr. Macgregor's Burnt Oak field. I knew the field was empty; it is being ploughed up for some experiment that Mr. Macgregor wants to try - blow all experiments! And to-day he gave his men a holiday to come and see the balloon. We were about fifteen hundred feet up and going slowly. I could see the oak and its shadow quite plainly. So I let the stone drop."

Hugh paused again and groaned.

"Go on," said somebody.

"No one noticed what I had done, but something or other made Mr. Ferguson start talking about how dangerous it was to chuck things over carelessly, though it seems to me that in Jules Verne they spend half their time chucking sandbags about. I asked him how about a stone weighing half a pound, and he said it would fall half a mile in twelve and a half seconds, and if it hit anyone on the head that person would be as dead as if he had got a bullet through him. I felt a bit

The Happy Adventurers

199

sick, but I was glad that field had been empty. We came down soon after that, and I cut off to Burnt Oak field to look for my stone." Hugh stopped short.

"Go on," said the others.

"It wasn't there, nor anywhere round; and I *knew* it must have dropped on that field."

"But," said Jerry, "if it hit the earth at that speed it would bury itself ever so deep. You could not possibly see it."

"I thought of that," said Hugh, "so I looked for the hole, and I found it. About thirty feet from the tree, which was a good hit considering. I could soon learn to aim well - that is, if I'm not hanged or sent to prison for life. Oh - Well, I found the hole, and beside it I found -"

No one dared to ask a question. Hugh remained silent till it was almost more than they could bear.

"Blood!" he whispered at last.

"Jiminy! Is that all!" exclaimed Dick. "I thought you were going to say a dead body. If the body got up and walked away it couldn't have been so very dead. How much blood? Were there any footmarks about?"

"That part of the field hadn't been ploughed, and the ground was rather hard, covered with grass the cattle had been cropping. There were some stones in a little pile, but my stone wasn't among them. I looked at those stones - by George, I looked at them! They were splashed with blood - Then I got sick, and then had to skedaddle because someone was calling me."

"I am *sure* it will turn out all right; you had the lucky diamond," Grizzel said consolingly.

"That makes it worse," said Hugh, groaning again. "I tied the diamond up with the stone and forgot to take it out."

"Oh, *Hugh*!" exclaimed Prudence, more perturbed by this disaster than by the hypothetical murder, "how *could* you be so careless?"

"It doesn't matter," Grizzel persisted, with cheerful calm, "that diamond brings luck. It has had one miracle, and I expect it will have another. It will come back. Very likely the dead man will bring it back himself."

"It will come back all right," said Hugh, "because the ring has Grizzel's name inside it, and, seeing that mine is the same on the handkerchief, the police will have a jolly good clue to start on. If the person was *not* hit and steals the diamond he'll take good care not to show himself. Then the diamond will be gone, but I'll give Grizzel mine. I'll spend my bank money on getting a ring made. Oh - if I only knew! If I only knew what was going to happen I shouldn't mind so much. It's waiting for that bobby to turn up that gives me the horrors." He looked over his shoulder as he spoke, with a shiver of anticipation.

"It sounds to me a bit fishy, you know," said Jerry, with a thoughtful frown. "How do you know that the hole you saw was made by your stone? It might have been there already."

"Because it was fresh, and the earth round was freshly thrown up; and some of my handkerchief was lying beside it."

The boys looked grave. This did sound rather serious.

"But," said Mollie, "the stone could not have buried itself in a hole and hit a person so that the person was killed at the same time. If it went down into a hole it did not hit anyone."

"I never thought of that," said Hugh, cheering up for the first time. "Neither it could; but there was the blood," he added despondently, "pints of it. I never thought anything could bleed so much. Well - I shall know before very long one way or the other, for either some news will turn up or the diamond will stay away."

"The best thing you can do now is to have some tea," said Prudence, "then you will feel better and we can plan what to do."

Things certainly looked less black after tea. Hugh, beginning to hope for Grizzel's miracle, decided to develop some photographs of the ballooners which he had taken on the previous day. "I promised Mr. Ferguson to have some prints ready for him to-morrow," he said, "so I may as well begin. If the bobby comes you can call me."

But everyone wanted to watch the developing process. Hugh's dark-room was a roomy lean-to shed, built by himself and well equipped with shelves, sink, and taps. It would hold six people at a pinch.

"No, I can't have you all," Hugh said, "you wouldn't all see at once, and it is too much of a crowd. I'll take two at a time. Dick and Prue to begin with."

The remaining three settled themselves within sight of the garden gate, and discussed the various features of Hugh's adventure.

"I don't believe it is half so bad as he thinks," Jerry said, "because it stands to reason that a dead man could not get up and walk away, especially not across a ploughed field. I doubt if even a man who had lost several pints of blood could walk very far. And if he had been *carried* off, there would have been a fuss, and the ballooners would have been tackled at once - in fact, I can't think why they weren't. I think it looks rather bad for Grizzel's diamond; worse for the diamond than for the man. I wonder how fast the balloon was going. How fast does a balloon fly?"

"Somewhere from eight to thirty-six miles an hour, according to the wind, Jules Verne says," Grizzel answered.

"Eight miles an hour! My hat! Fancy crawling through the air at eight -"

There was a sound at the garden gate and the three jumped to their feet. A young man walked up the broad path between the cypress trees, striking across the grass when he saw the children. He was not a policeman, having indeed a very kind and cheerful expression, which he was trying, not very successfully, to hide under a severe frown.

" Does anyone named Grizzel Campbell live in this

house?" he asked.

"Yes, me," Grizzel answered, turning a little pale.

"You!" exclaimed the young man, looking with some astonishment at the small figure before him, with its tumbled red curls. "I don't suppose *you* are the owner of a -" he broke off uncertainly.

"She is the owner of a green diamond in a ring, if that is what you wish to know," Jerry spoke up.

"What on earth is a kid like you doing with a magnificent diamond ring?" the young man asked, forgetting to frown and letting everyone see quite plainly what a nice face he really had.

"Oh - have you got my ring? Has there been a miracle?" Grizzel cried, clutching at the young man's arm.

"I have got the ring, and there has been a miracle sure enough," he answered rather grimly. "I suppose that Mr. Hugh Campbell is your brother. Where is he?"

"He's here all right," Jerry answered, "but would you mind telling us what happened before I call him? Whatever he did he's jolly cut up about it, and if it was anything very bad I'd like to - to prepare him a bit, you know. He went to look for his stone and got the fright of his life when he found his hank and the blood."

"Blood!" the young man ejaculated, with a puzzled frown. "What blood?"

" He said the ground was soaked in blood. All the

stones were red. He thinks that the person he hit must have lost pints of blood."

The young man threw back his head and laughed - a big, reassuring laugh which brought some colour into the three pale and anxious faces turned up to his. "Blood! I see! No, it was not so bad as all that, it only *might* have been. It was not blood, it was only - but I'd better begin at the beginning and tell you what happened. I was sitting in Macgregor's Burnt Oak field, working at - well, a little experiment I am interested in, when I saw the balloon had come right over. Of course I had been watching it, but for a bit I was absorbed in my experiment and had not looked up. I looked up then and was staring hard, when suddenly, before I could say Jack Robinson, a whacking stone came hurtling down and cleared my head by less than a foot. If it had hit me - by Jove! I'd have tried the last and biggest experiment before this!"

"A foot is a pretty good miss," said Jerry, a look of immense relief spreading over his face. "I know a chap who had a parting cut in his hair with a bullet; that's what *I* call a narrow shave. That's what he calls it too," Jerry added, with a grin.

"No doubt he does. My shave was narrow enough for me, thank you. It all but knocked my precious experiment into the middle of next week. But what I want to know is why Hugh Campbell throws diamond rings about the country. If the stone hadn't plopped into the middle of my - my little game - which was almost another miracle when you consider the size of the field - the ring would have been lost for ever."

" It's a miraculous ring, " Grizzel explained, "and it

brings luck. I expect you'll be ever so lucky now. But how did you know where to look for Hugh?" she added rather anxiously. Mr. Ferguson would not be pleased, to put it mildly, if he knew how nearly Hugh had involved him in a tragedy.

"I know your father," the young man replied, "he once did me a good turn. So I knew where to look for the owner of the handkerchief without troubling Mr. Ferguson."

"But what was that mush if it wasn't blood?" asked Jerry.

"That? Oh - that was merely my little experiment; that is my secret for the present, and I trust you not to mention it. But no one has told me why your brother chucked a diamond ring out of the balloon."

"It was a mistake; he was trying experiments too," Grizzel explained. "But, please, may I go and tell him that he isn't a murderer? He is expecting to be hanged every minute, and it makes him feel perfectly miserable. But I was sure that my ring would bring him luck."

Grizzel sped off on her mission. She knocked at the dark-room door. "Please put an ear at the keyhole - I have important news."

An ear was promptly at her disposal. She did not ask whose, but went on:

"The murdered man has come, and he isn't in the least dead. And his blood wasn't blood, only his experiment, and he's got my ring. He is a nice man, and he is

Lydia Miller Middleton

forgiving Hugh as hard as he can, and there were two miracles, and I told you so!"

There was a momentary silence within, and then a glad shout. Dick began to sing "God save the King", which seemed less appropriate when he remembered that the sovereign of the moment was a queen; but no one noticed, and the main point was that someone was saved. A few minutes later the dark-room party emerged, Hugh very pale and shaky as he went to meet his supposed victim. Indeed, for a moment he was incapable of speech, and Jerry, who knew only too well what it felt like to have a lump sticking in his throat just when he wanted to be most manly and soldier-like, filled up what would have been an awkward pause by saying anything that came into his head until Hugh had recovered himself.

"I've had a lesson," he began, as he shook hands with the young man, whose name they now learnt was Desmond O'Rourke. "I am awfully sorry -"

"That's all right," Mr. O'Rourke interrupted, "we all have to learn lessons now and then - I've learnt some myself - at least I hope I have. How are the photographs turning out?"

"Very well, thank you. Would you like to come and see them? Mr. Ferguson's is the best portrait I have done yet." Hugh recovered from his emotion as he spoke, but he was still very pale.

Mr. O'Rourke accepted the invitation with alacrity. "We can exchange experiences," he said. "I am curious to know what the experiment was that so nearly bowled me out. But first I must return the diamond to its owner." He drew the ring out of an inner pocket and held it out to Grizzel. As the diamond met the golden glow of the fading day its green rays gleamed and sparkled. "One might believe it was alive!" Mr. O'Rourke exclaimed. "I never saw anything like it. You kids ought not to have a jewel like that to play pitch-and-toss with; someone should keep it for you."

"I wear it round my neck," said Grizzel, unfastening the neckband of her overall and showing a slender chain of finely wrought gold. She took it off and slung the ring on.

"I have one almost as good," Hugh observed, as they watched Grizzel, "but mine is not set yet; perhaps I'll have it made into a ring some day. Mamma says I should keep it till I want an engagement ring -"

"O bay o' Dublin, my heart you're troublin',"

Mollie gave a violent start - but it was only Bridget singing in the kitchen.

Mr. O'Rourke turned his head and listened. "Who comes from Dublin?" he asked.

"It's Bridget, our nurse when Baby is here and our cook just now," Prudence answered. "She's feeling homesick. She does sometimes."

"So do I," said Mr. O'Rourke. "It's a long time since I've seen the bay o' Dublin. I must shake hands with Bridget."

Mollie gazed earnestly at Mr. O'Rourke. Was *he* Aunt Mary's long-ago lover? No - he was too old. He must be twenty-two at least. But she felt almost sure that *somehow* he had something to do with that romance.

As they stood at the white gate later on, saying good-bye, their new friend pulled a round white stone out of one of his many pockets. "Shall I keep this or shall I give it to you?" he asked Hugh.

There was a curious silence as the children gathered round to gaze at the innocent-looking missile in Mr. O'Rourke's hand. It was little the worse of its adventure - slightly chipped and scratched, and on one side an ominous red stain which made Hugh shiver and turn pale again, as it reminded him how nearly his thoughtlessness had cost a life.

"Give it to me," he said at last. "I will write the date on it, and if it doesn't remind me to think twice, nothing will, and I will *deserve* to be hanged."

"Very well," agreed Mr. O'Rourke, "only remember that the red stain is only what I told you it was."

"I'll remember," said Hugh, holding the stone in his hand and looking gravely down at it, "but I won't forget that it *might* have been what I thought it was."

Grizzel's solemn round eyes went from one to the other during this transaction. "Is that what it means in books when it says, 'marked with a white stone'?" she asked Hugh.

"It *is* a sort of milestone," Hugh answered thoughtfully, "and it will mark a new start for me. It ought to have your name on as well as mine," he added, looking up at Mr. O'Rourke. "Perhaps it means a new mile for you too. You can't tell."

The young man laughed: "You make me feel as if it were my tombstone; you are all so solemn. Let me see a smile before I go."

A nice white smile flashed round the company, but Hugh's eyes remained thoughtful as he watched the young Irishman walk away down the leafy road.

After all the emotions of that exciting day Hugh was tired, so next morning found the children sitting quietly in the broad veranda. Prudence busied herself with sewing; Grizzel sat at the table happily absorbed in painting a spray of wattle to send to Mamma. She had placed it in a tall, slender vase of Venetian glass, pale yellow flecked with gold. Hugh lay on the floor, his chin in the hollow of his hands, and his feet alternately tapping the red bricks and waving in the air, as he contemplated a small steam-engine which he had been putting through its paces. Mollie, Dick, and Jerry sat on the veranda steps, the boys printing photographs, while Mollie idly played with the trailing garlands of morning-glory and traveller's joy which hung around her. Between the blossoming almond trees she could see golden splashes of wattle in the field beyond. At her feet a mass of big Russian violets boldly lifted their heads above their leaves, and an acacia, which overshadowed the veranda, was dropping milky petals on the path. Mollie knew all the sweet scents by name now. It was queer, she thought, how the seasons came slipping round, each bringing its own fruit and flowers - here in Australia in Prue's Time, and there in Chauncery in her own Time. She turned her head and stared at the shabby old grandfather clock which stood in a corner of the veranda. For forty years, she thought, its pendulum would slowly swing, till it said "How d'ye do" to the ticking clock in Grannie's morning-room. Forty years was a long time to look forward to.

"Jolly nice smells here," Dick remarked. "How ripping the almond blossom looks in the sunshine. We've got an almond tree in our backyard, and once there was an almond on it."

"There are thousands of almonds here," Prue said, pausing in her work for a moment and gazing dreamily at the delicate outline of almond branches against the sky. "They are nicest when they are green, but I must say they do give you dreadful pains. I wonder why so many nice things leave a pain. Music does too - and even one's best friends sometimes."

"Do you eat your best friends boiled up with green almonds to the tune of 'Good-bye for ever - good-bye, good-bye'?" Dick inquired.

They laughed. "There's an old gentleman come to live next door," Prudence continued, taking up her sewing again, "who watches us through a telescope some-times, and when he sees us in the green-almond trees he writes to Papa. He says it is for our good, old telltale. Once, though, he took us into his library and showed us some beautiful fossils. He said they were as old as Moses, and one of them might be a million years old. It was a fan-shell, quite whole and pretty. Fancy a million years! I wonder what the world will be like in another million years."

"Bust," said Dick briefly.

They laughed again and then were silent. Mollie

looked round at the little group and thought how easy it was to be good when one had nice things to do and plenty of time and room to do them in. "Where is Miss Hilton?" she asked, "and where is Laddie? And why aren't you at school this time? How do you ever learn enough to pass your exams?"

"Miss Hilton is housekeeper while Mamma is away," Prudence answered, "and she hasn't much time for lessons. Laddie is dead. He was poisoned. We couldn't bear to have another dog. Papa doesn't like exams. He likes us to be out all the time and not to stoop over books. He says we can 'find tongues in trees, books in the running brooks, sermons in stones, and good in everything'."

Mollie gave a little jump. The very words Aunt Mary had quoted that morning! There was certainly *something* queer somewhere!

"What a jolly kind of father to have," Dick exclaimed. "I wish my good parent held these views. His are quite otherwise. He believes in any amount of stooping over books, though I am always pointing out to him that it isn't the chaps who swot over books that turn into Generals and things in the end."

"When Mamma comes home Grizzel and I are going to school." Prudence said regretfully. "I know we shall hate it, but I suppose we must learn grammar and geography some time." She sighed at the distressing prospect before her.

Mollie smiled as she wondered what school would make of Grizzel. She looked at Hugh, absorbed in some great new idea. What would he be like in forty

Lydia Miller Middleton

years. In Chauncery Time he must now be fifty-four. Were there then *two* Hughs? And if two, why not twenty? Or hundreds, for that matter, like the films of a cinematograph. Perhaps everyone had a sort of film-picture running off all the time, and some day, before those million years had passed, a way would be found to develop them. It would not be much more wonderful than wireless and flying and all those things that looked impossible to people in this Time. Mollie began to think of London, and of home in North Kensington, and then felt a sudden longing for her mother and Jean and the little ones - for all the familiar ways of home and school. This place was lovely, and the children were perfect dears, but it would be nice to feel a hockey-stick in her hand again - and she *should* like to see her own comfortable mother. In fact, she felt homesick!

"A balloon is all very well," Hugh said, "so far as it goes." He rolled round on to his back, clasping his hands under his head and staring up at the white clouds over which he had flown yesterday. "But it doesn't go far *enough*. It will never be much use until we learn to steer. You have to go whichever way the wind chooses, which may be exactly the way you don't want to go. I can't see myself how one could ever steer without machinery, and to carry that weight you'd have to have a balloon the size of a mountain."

"There's wings," said Prudence, "like Hiram Brown."

"What's the good of wings that let you drop the moment you try to fly with them. Hiram Brown is as dead as a door nail with his wings. No, wings fastened on *that* way will never work. Our internal machinery isn't made like birds'." As he spoke a parrot flew overhead, its brilliant wings flashing in the sunlight and then becoming apparently motionless as it swooped down towards the house. Hugh's eyes followed it intently, and presently he rolled over again and resumed his study of the steam-engine.

"Wings," he murmured, "after all wings are the right things to fly with. Why not make the whole thing, body and all." He frowned hard as he concentrated his whole attention upon the toy before him. "Wings - and steam - a boiler -"

The boys and Mollie watched him curiously. This was the Thought that came before the Thing, Mollie thought, remembering her conversation with Aunt Mary. It was rather like a game of hide-and-seek. Hugh was getting warm - how near would he get? They tried to catch the disjointed words that fell from his lips at intervals. "Wings," he muttered again, "and a place for the flier - why not a car - a - a - a box like an engine-driver's, with handles for controlling -"

In the minds of the English children, now listening breathlessly, there arose a vividly distinct image of an aeroplane, darkly silhouetted against a pale English sky. How many they had seen!

Hugh's mutterings ceased. It seemed to Mollie that the world had grown very still. She fancied that she could almost hear the blossoms dropping on the grass; there was a faint stir of leaves as a stray breeze came wandering by, and another sound mingled with that stir - a far-away hum - hum - growing louder every moment!

The English children looked at each other. Was this

one of Grizzel's miracles? Their eyes turned to the sky - yes, there it came! It winged its way like a mighty bird, singing its strange rough song. Prue dropped her work and stood up, Grizzel let fall her pencil and clung to Prue, Hugh leapt to his feet and ran down the steps, his face upturned to the clouds.

"Oh, what is it?" he cried. "What is it? Who are you?"

The aeroplane swooped down as the bird had done, till it was straight overhead, then, with a lovely curve, it skimmed away, the great wings outstretched as the bird's had been, away into the distant blue!

Hugh held out his arms. "Don't go - oh, don't go!" he cried. "Come back, come back!"

But it had gone.

The English children looked at each other again, and from each other to Hugh.

"*We* brought it," whispered Jerry, "it was a Time-traveller."

Mollie turned to the Australians. The sunlight fell on Hugh's pale face, on Grizzel's ruddy curls; there was a faint smile on Prue's lips.

"Oh, we have brought our Time too near," she exclaimed. "It is good-bye! No, no, Prue! Oh - *this* time it is good-bye!"

*   *   *   *   *

" No, no - I don't want to wake up yet! It is too soon! I

haven't said good-bye. Not yet, Aunt Mary!"

"It's not 'good-bye', my Mollie, it's 'how d'ye do?' you've got to say! You have been dreaming too hard, child."

Mollie sat up and rubbed her eyes in bewilderment, for it was not Aunt Mary at all, but Mother, standing there and smiling.

"No, it's not my ghost," she laughed, when Mollie had released her stranglehold. "I came down partly to see how my daughterling was getting along, and partly to ask Grannie and Aunt Mary if they would like two more troublesome, non-paying guests. Would it bore you unutterably to have to entertain your twin and Jerry Outram for a fortnight?"

"Oh, Mother! Not really! How perfectly lovely! Why?"

"Measles at school; so they are closing a month early, and it would be *such* a boon to Mrs. Outram and me if the boys could be quarantined away from home. Aunt Mary says she would *like* to have them, strange woman, and Grannie is already planning a course of Manners - the beautiful capital-M Manners of her young days."

Mollie laughed as she gave her mother a comfortable unmannerly hug. "You are all frauds," she said. "Don't talk to me of your young days. I guess they weren't one pin better than ours. I hope Dick and Jerry are coming soon."

"To-morrow. Now, I'll have some tea, and then a little talk, and then I must be off again. I stole Father's car,

Lydia Miller Middleton

as he has gone down to Bournemouth. So there's no time to waste. What beautiful strawberries!"

"They are ready just in time for the boys," said Grannie benignly.

CHAPTER VIII

How it Ended

Dick and Jerry arrived on the following morning in rampageous spirits. To get away from hot and dusty London to the cool, green country, from the discipline and restrictions of school to the benevolent and generous rule of Grannie's household, from plain bread-and-butter, stews, and solid puddings, to Martha's delicious scones and unlimited strawberries and cream - was enough to make any thirteen-year-old schoolboy radiantly cheerful. There was plenty to do at Chauncery, too; a first-class tennis-court and an aunt who played for her county; excellent golf and the same aunt nearly as good at golf as she was at tennis; a pony to be ridden or driven, several dogs and a new litter of puppies, and last but not least, Mollie, and the mystery of the Time-travellers to be talked over.

"Here we are, Grannie," Dick exclaimed superfluously, running up the front steps to where Grannie stood with a smile of welcome on her beaming face. "And jolly glad to be here, you bet your best Sunday bonnet. London is like a baker's oven. You look very fit, Grannie, and Jerry says Aunt Mary is too young to be my aunt; I believe he is spoons on her already - what ho! my Uncle Jerry! Come and be introduced." Dick gave Jerry's arm a tug, and Young Outram shook hands

Lydia Miller Middleton

with a smile that won Grannie's heart at once.

Mollie had limped out of the morning-room with the help of a stout crook-handled stick. Dick gave her a brotherly peck, and Jerry looked at her commiseratingly. It was rather difficult to reconcile this pale, limping Mollie with the active young Time-traveller of yesterday.

"You're looking a bit like a mashed potato," Dick remarked critically. "You've been shut up in the house too much. It's time we came and hauled you out. I'll tell you what, Aunt Polly-wolly-doodle, we'll take her out for a drive in the trap this afternoon."

"We'll see," said Aunt Mary. "I am afraid you are too fresh, Dick. You might tumble her out in the exuberance of your spirits. Besides, it is going to rain - it is drizzling already."

"Pouf!" said Dick lightly. "What's a little rain! A little soft, wet rain will do her good. And Long John seems to have been eating his fat head off; he played no end of jinks coming along just now. I'll take him round to the stables - I want to see the puppies. Hop in, Moll. We'll bring you back in a queen's chair."

But Grannie insisted upon some light refreshment first. She was sure the boys must be exhausted after their two hours' journey from town. "And the best way to fight measles is to feed you up," she said, leading the way to the dining-room, where strawberries, cherries, biscuits, and a jug of creamy milk stood invitingly upon the table.

The boys consented to the feeding-up process without

a murmur. When the plates were all empty they departed on a round of visits to the stable, tennis-court, tool-shed, and other haunts dear to the heart of boy. Aunt Mary firmly refused to allow Mollie to accompany them, even in the queen's chair they offered.

"You are tired already," she said to her niece, "and if you want to go for that drive this afternoon you must certainly rest first. Back to your sofa, Miss Mollie - away with you!"

So Mollie rested, with a book in her lap and her thoughts by turns far away and near home.

Later on she was carefully helped into the little governess-cart, with a list of messages to be done in the village, and another list of extravagant promises from the boys of the amazing benefits she was to derive from her outing with them. Long John had got over his first fine raptures, and was now willing to jog along the sweet country lanes at a steady and sober pace, suitable for the invalid he carried behind him.

"How jolly nice it does look after London," Jerry remarked, as a long branch of honeysuckle swept his cap on to the floor of the trap, where he let it lie unconcernedly. "After all - there's no place like old England. For looks, anyhow."

> "Each to his choice, and I rejoice
> The lot has fallen to me
> In a fair ground - in a fair ground -
> Yea, Sussex by the sea,"

Mollie quoted, as they came to a standstill at the top of

Lydia Miller Middleton

a long incline. In the distance they saw the sea gleaming somewhat greyly under a brief spell of sunshine. All around them the trees and hedges sparkled with raindrops, green and cool and wet.

"They look like green diamonds," said Dick, letting his cap drop beside Jerry's and allowing the reins to fall loosely on Long John's back, as the pony edged to the side of the road and began to nibble the grass. "Rather different from the gold-diggings, isn't it?"

This remark set the ball rolling. "What do you think it was?" Mollie began.

"Blessed if I know," Dick answered, with a shake of his head, "blue magic of some sort. Unless we all dreamt it."

"No, it wasn't a dream," said Jerry thoughtfully. "It was simply psychical phenomena. I've heard of things just as queer. Awfully funny things happen in India. And look at the 'phantom armies' in France."

"Rot," said Dick briefly. "*I* think it was a kink in Mollie's brain, and she passed it on to me. We do, sometimes. Mother says all twins do. And your silly head was as empty as usual and you psychicked it from me."

"Rot," said Jerry, with as much decision as Dick. "I saw the blooming parrot as soon as you did, if not sooner."

"It wasn't rot," Mollie said decidedly; "whatever it was it wasn't rot. *I* think -" she paused for a moment to consider her words - "I believe it may have been just what Prue said it was. We travelled back in Time. It sounds impossible, but if you come to think of it lots of things that happen now would have sounded impossible to those children, or at any rate to Papa and Mamma. If Alice in Wonderland could have seen forty years ahead she would have found it quite easy to believe six impossible things before breakfast. There's submarines for one, and flying, and wireless, especially telephones, and the cinema. If we could have taken the Campbells to a moving picture of a submarine submerging, with aeroplanes flying round, and a lecture wirelessed from America coming out of a gramophone, and the music done with a piano-player, Time-travelling would not have seemed much more wonderful to them."

Dick shook his head again. "It's different," he said. "All those things might have seemed very wonderful and *almost* impossible, but they weren't *quite* impossible. Time-travelling is."

"But we've done it," said Mollie.

Nobody answered. There did not appear to be an answer to that statement.

"Have you ever heard," Mollie said at last, speaking slowly and looking at the boys with solemn eyes, "of a thing called Einstein's Theory of Relatittey - I mean Rela*tiv*ity - Rel-a-*tiv*-ity?"

"Old Bibs jawed us about it one day," Dick answered, "but he said no one could understand it except the chap himself and not always him. So he didn't expect us to, which was a good job for everybody."

"That's what Aunt Mary said; I heard her talking. That's why I read about it, because I'm fairly good at maths. She has it all pasted in a book. I had to skip most of it, but here and there I found bits. I took some notes," Mollie drew a penny notebook from her pocket. "One man says that, if the world travelled as fast as light, there would be no Time. All the clocks would stop, and we'd be There as soon as we were Here. Well now, that's just what we did. We were Here - and we were There. So our time stopped and Now was Then. See?"

"He says *If*. You couldn't live without Time. You *must* have Time to do things in or where would you be? You'd have to swallow all the meals of your life at one mouthful and you'd bust. What comes next?"

"Another man says," Mollie read impressively, "that any schoolboy - *any* schoolboy," she repeated, fixing a stern eye upon her brother, "can see that, if the velocity of light has a given value with reference to the fixed stars, it cannot have the same value with reference to its source when this is moved relatively to the stars."

"Gee-whiz!" said Dick. "Next, please."

"A man says that perhaps things measured north and south are different from things measured east and west. *We* travelled north and south. Perhaps we stretched back in Time all of a sudden, like elastic."

"Couldn't be done. Elastic stretches both ways. If *you* tried to move north and south both at the same time you'd go off like a Christmas cracker. Next."

"A man says that our ideas of space and time may be

all wrong."

"Aunt Polly will agree with him if we stand here much longer," said Dick. "Next. Hurry up."

"You don't stop to *think*," Mollie said impatiently. "Try and *think*. Your head might just as well be a football. What *I* think is that if two un-understandable things are discovered about the same time they must belong to each other. Don't you see *that*?"

"They might," Dick said cautiously, "and then again they mightn't. I don't think myself that there's any use trying to understand things like Time-travelling and Relativity. People like us never will."

"I don't know that," said Jerry, who had been listening to the discussion in silence.

"There's lots of things just as hard to understand, only you take them for granted. Being alive, for instance. Look at Mollie fidgeting about, and Long John chewing and twitching, and the trees waving their branches, and you shaking your head as if it were a dinner-bell, which is about what it is - it's all life. Just as hard to understand as Relativity, and a jolly sight harder if you ask me. I can't say I understand Time-travelling, but - " Jerry broke off.

Mollie frowned thoughtfully. "We don't understand it *yet*," she said, "but in *another* forty years -"

They were all silent. Another forty years!

"We'll be fifty-three," Dick said at last. "A jolly funny looking lot we'll be. All sitting round staring at each other through specs, with white hair and no teeth worth mentioning. I'll have an ear-trumpet, and Mollie will wear a cap like Grannie's, and Jerry will be a blithering old idiot saying, 'Hey!' like General Dyson-Polks."

They had to laugh at this picture of themselves, and then Mollie began at the beginning and told the story of Prue's first visit. The boys were deeply interested. Their own experiences had merely been a repetition of the first - Hugh had appeared and, like the gentleman who dealt in Relativity, they were Here and they were There. "It has taught us something about Australia anyhow," said Dick; "that is, of course, if we saw the real thing. The next thing is to find out whether we did or if the whole show was just bunkum."

"What I should like to know," said Jerry reflectively, "is who the Campbells were, and how they got mixed up with your lot. They must have at some time, or your people wouldn't have those photographs."

Mollie smiled. She knew how they and the Campbells had got "mixed up", but she had never told the boys of her discovery; it was a little secret between her and a certain photograph that smiled down at her from the morning-room mantelpiece. She liked to think how the original would have laughed along with her.

"What I should like to know," said Dick, "is what that chap O'Rourke was doing in that field. What was his mysterious experiment, and how did Hugh's stone cut into it? That's what I want to know, and I don't suppose I ever will, now. I don't think we'll go back, not at present anyway. The show's over for this time. In fact I don't want to go; I'm too jolly well pleased to be where I am. Gee-up, you lazy brute," - this to Long John, who apparently thought he had done enough work for one day and was nosing about the soft grass with contemptuous disregard for his passengers. He moved on unwillingly, and Dick took him briskly downhill.

In the village there were old friends to be greeted, and many inquiries for Mollie's ankle to be answered. Fresh crusty loaves were brought out by the baker, loosely wrapped in soft paper, and packed away under the seats. A large box, containing a peculiarly delicious make of sponge cake, was set on Mollie's lap, and a blue paper bag of sifted sugar was entrusted to Jerry's special care by a misguided grocer. Dick had a golf-club needing attention, which entailed a long and intimate conversation with the local carpenter, who was also a well-known local golfer, and the best hand at repairing clubs, Dick was convinced, in the whole of Great Britain.

It was getting on towards tea-time when Long John's head was at last turned homewards, and his feet covered the ground with cheerful and approving swiftness. A drizzle of rain fell, "Just enough to save us the trouble of washing for tea," Dick commented. "Do you think our white aunt can be induced to come and play golf after tea, Moll, or is she afraid of rain?"

"Good gracious, no," Mollie replied. "Aunt Mary goes out in all the weathers ever invented. She will love a round of golf; she hasn't played since I sprained my ankle. I wish I could come too. I wonder if I could hop round with my stick and look on. I do love to watch Aunt Mary drive; I learnt a lot from her last week before I sprained my ankle in that idiotic way."

The boys negatived this proposal. "You'd get a ball in

the eye to finish you up with," Dick said. "We'll plan some picnics till you are better, and explore the country a bit and knock some fat off this animal - hullo! - what's that?"

A sudden twist in the narrow road had brought into view a motor bicycle, leaning dejectedly against the hedge, whilst its owner squatted beside it and tinkered at its mechanism - tinkered in vain apparently, for, as the boys drew up beside him to offer assistance, he rose to his feet and shook his head hopelessly.

"Can we help you?" Dick asked, eyeing the bicycle with interest. "I'm afraid we've got no tools here, but there is a smithy about a mile farther on and the chap there has a motor bike, so I expect he could lend you a hand."

"Thank you very much," replied the stranger, looking relieved. "I'll shove her along there and leave her. I am much afraid she's gone altogether phut for the time being, and will have to be trundled back to town by rail. Can you tell me if I am anywhere near a place called Chauncery?"

"Rather," Dick answered, with a grin. "That's our place. It's about half a mile up the next turning to the left."

"Indeed!" said the stranger, looking somewhat surprised and slightly dismayed; "I understood that it was occupied by Mrs. and Miss Gordon, not by anyone with chil - young people," he corrected himself hastily.

"So it is. But at present they've got us, owing to circs. We are Mrs. Gordon's grandchildren."

"Oh - I see! I hope that Mrs. and Miss Gordon are in good health?"

"Pretty bobbish, thank you," Dick was answering when Mollie interrupted:

"Can we give you a lift? We are on our way home, and I am sure it is going to rain hard presently."

"That is a very kind offer," the motorist replied gratefully, "and I wish I could accept it, as I am a trifle lame; but I can't very well leave my machine lying derelict by the roadside, and I fear that your hospitality cannot be extended to the old bus, I thought perhaps - if you would be so very kind - you might drop a message at the smithy you mentioned, and I will wait here until they send someone along."

But the word "lame" had roused all Mollie's sympathy. "How lame are you?" she asked. "Is it a wound? I am lame too - only a sprained ankle, but I should hate to walk from here to Chauncery."

"Of course you couldn't," the motorist said kindly. "I am not so bad as that. My wound healed long ago, but it has left rather a crocky foot behind. I could manage well enough, however, if someone from the smithy would come and push the bike."

"Tell you what," Dick suggested; "if you hop in and look after Mollie, Jerry and I will push the bike to the smithy; we'll be after you in two jiffs."

The stranger looked at Dick with a smile and a slight lift of his eyebrows. "You are very trusting, young man. Supposing I run away with the pony and the cart and the sister? What will you do then?"

"Stick to the bike," Dick answered promptly, "I have been wanting one most frightfully badly, and Father says I might as well ask him to give me the Isle of Wight. Besides - you *said* you knew Grannie and Aunt Mary."

"Well, I happen to be quite a safe person, so you're all right this time, but it wouldn't *always* do, you know," and the stranger gave his head a warning shake. "You are exceedingly kind. I only fear it would be rather a heavy job for you."

But this the boys denied strenuously. "If we stick, one of us will go and collect young Simpson and the other will watch the bike; but we'll be as right as rain - and we'd better hurry up." Dick left the trap as he spoke by the simple means of dropping over the side, and Jerry followed his example.

"I had better give you my name for Mr. - Simpson, did you say? - Major Campbell - Hugh Campbell."

There was a dead silence. If the stranger had said "George the Fifth of England" he could not have produced more effect. All three stared at him with their mouths open. "What's the matter with that?" he asked. "It's a very respectable name, and it really does belong to me. Perhaps I should give you my card." He put his hand in his breastpocket.

"Oh no," Mollie said rather breathlessly. "No - please don't mind - it's quite all right, only - you look so young."

"So *what*?" exclaimed Major Campbell, standing stock still with his hand in his pocket.

"I mean," Mollie explained nervously, "I mean -" looking at the boys for help, but in vain, "I - you - so young to be a friend of Grannie's" she ended feebly.

"You're a goose, Moll," Dick broke in. "We once knew a Hugh Campbell, but it was years and *years* ago, and he was ever so much younger than you - he was my age - and there must be thousands of Hugh Campbells."

"Years and years ago! Your age! And she says I look too young!" repeated Major Campbell in pardonable bewilderment. "How old do I look - five perhaps?"

Mollie blushed, and the boys giggled. "Look here," said Dick, "if we stand here till midnight discussing Major Campbell's age we won't get home to tea, and then Aunt Mary will send out a search party, and we'll look pretty asinine. Long John's getting baity, he'll bolt in a minute. Take the reins, Mollie. Don't eat all the strawberries, and tell Aunt Mary that cherry jam is my fancy. Come on, Young Outram."

Major Campbell saw the boys start before taking the reins from Mollie. Long John gave his head an impatient toss, and set off with the determination that he would not stop again for anybody till he was in sight of his stable.

A hundred thoughts chased each other through Mollie's mind. Of course this could not possibly be *that* Hugh Campbell. It would be altogether *too* queer. And yet - after all, nothing could be much queerer than the experience they had already had. Putting one thing and another together it did seem to be more than a coincidence that a Hugh Campbell should be on his way to see someone who had a green diamond set in a ring given to her "long, long ago". She stole a look at her companion as he sat opposite her, his eyes fixed on the road ahead and his thoughts obviously elsewhere. Hugh the inventor had not passed even thirteen years without gathering various little mementoes of his inventions in the shape of scars here and there, and these had not escaped the sharp observation of Mollie, the Girl Guide. There had been a tiny gap in his left eyebrow, the result of inventing a new pattern of firework - a crooked little finger on his left hand - a funny star-shaped mark on his right jaw. Some of these and other remembered marks might have been obliterated by time, but if even one remained she would recognize it. He had removed his hat and disclosed a head of closely cropped grey hair, which made him look older. Yes - there was the gap in his eyebrow *and* the crooked finger. Mollie felt certain that this was indeed the inventor.

"Have you ever been in Dublin?" she asked abruptly, forgetting for the moment that asking questions was forbidden.

"In Dublin?" echoed Major Campbell, bringing his eyes and his thoughts from the winding road and concentrating both upon Mollie. "Are you a thought-reader, Miss Mollie? For I was thinking of Dublin at that very moment. Yes, I have been there. Indeed, it was there that I first met Miss Gordon, at a ball at Dublin Castle. I was visiting some people she knew, and later on she joined us. My sisters were over here at that time too. Has Miss Gordon ever mentioned the

O'Rourkes to you?"

"Yes," said Mollie, feeling absolutely giddy with excitement, "that is, no - not exactly - " she felt very confused - "I mean - was there a Desmond O'Rourke?"

"That's right," said Major Campbell, nodding his grey head, and apparently too wrapped up in his own memories to notice Mollie's confused answer. "Good old Desmond! Of course he was home then too. Dublin was a very different place in those days, and we had what you youngsters would call the time of our lives. It was a long time ago - long, long ago." He sighed, and his thoughts evidently wandered away again from his agitated little companion, which Mollie felt was a good thing, as, if he had been observing her closely, he would certainly have thought that the poor child was "not *quite* on the spot".

She was now quite convinced that this was really Hugh, the brother of Prudence and Grizzel. He showed no signs of remembering her, but, of course, she said to herself, what was only yesterday to her was forty years ago to this elderly man - and, besides, perhaps the Time-travelling was all hers and Prue's and he was never really in it at all. "Like Alice in the Red King's dream," she thought vaguely. She felt sure, too, that it was he who had given Aunt Mary the green diamond long ago, though why he had never married her was past Mollie's power of understanding. Grown-up people did - and left undone - the most incomprehensible things. In the meantime she felt that she would like to give her aunt some sort of warning of the surprise in store, otherwise Aunt Mary might be *too much* surprised. Mollie herself hated with all her might and main showing her feelings before people - but *how* to prepare Aunt Mary! That was the difficulty. She put all her Guiding wits to work, but nothing feasible suggested itself. There was no boy to send ahead with a message, and, of course, she could not send Major Campbell himself. How on earth could she get even the slightest warning conveyed.

The had begun to climb the hill which led to Chauncery gate; Long John's enthusiasm cooled a little, and he dropped into a jogging zigzag walk. Major Campbell was looking about him with interest, "Just the way I did," Mollie thought - and then the idea came.

"I'm going to signal to Aunt Mary that we are nearly home," she warned her companion, "so that she'll have tea ready," and, putting her hands to her mouth, she gave a long, shrill "cooo-eeeee!" "Now," she said to herself, "that should remind her of Australia and Desmond O'Rourke and green diamonds."

But Mollie's brilliant idea had not exactly the effect she expected. When the sound of that shrill cooo-eeeee penetrated to the morning-room, Aunt Mary did indeed think of Australia, but she also thought, naturally enough, that the children were in difficulties and needed her help. So, a few minutes later, Mollie and Major Campbell saw a slim figure, clad in a short skirt and jumper, running down the hill as fast as a pair of active feet could carry it.

"Oh, *dear*!" Mollie exclaimed, "Aunt Mary thinks something is wrong, and when she sees no boys and you here instead she will think it is wronger."

"*That* can't be Mary Gordon!" exclaimed Major

Campbell. "She doesn't look much older than you!"

"It is, though," Mollie replied hurriedly, more flashes of genius scintillating through her brain. "Jump out and meet her, Major Campbell, and tell her we are all right."

This suggestion evidently met with entire approval, for Major Campbell, adopting Dick's tactics, was over the side of the cart and striding (with a slight limp) up the hill "Before you could say Jack Robinson," Mollie quoted, as she took the reins and tactfully directed Long John's attention to an extra juicy patch of grass. Between his greed and her excitement they nearly overturned into the ditch, but a kindly boulder saved them in the nick of time.

"I must say," Mollie soliloquized, "he is fairly old for Aunt Mary, though he doesn't look it even with that white hair. What *will* the boys say? I believe Aunt Mary has forgotten all about us - there they go! Up the hill without ever once looking at me. I suppose I may follow now. Gee-up, Long John. Don't you ever think of *anything* but eating?" (which was a little unfair of Mollie under the circumstances).

But if Aunt Mary had forgotten her family she very soon remembered it again, for she and Major Campbell were waiting at the gate when Mollie came up, and they all arrived at the front door together.

When Dick and Jerry came within sight of the house, the first thing to catch their eyes was Mollie at an upstairs window, and a pair of signalling flags going hard. The boys stopped short.

Lydia Miller Middleton

"It - is - Hugh. It - is - Hugh. It - is - Hugh," the flags repeated emphatically. "Look - out. With - Aunt - in drawing - room. Beware. Hurry - up."

"My aunt!" Dick exclaimed appropriately. "What the dickens does she mean? Aunt Mary and that old chap! Get out! His hair is whiter than Father's. Aunt Mary has got the hardest overhand serve in Sussex. *She* doesn't want to get married, I'll bet my boots. Rot!"

"I don't know that," said Jerry. "I rather twigged that when he asked for her. I believe that old Johnny *is* Hugh. I think he is a jolly decent-looking chap, and white hair means nothing nowadays. And after you're forty I don't see that it matters what age you are." Jerry was encouraging a romantic tenderness for Prue and her brown curls, consequently he felt slightly superior to Dick.

The boys left the tell-tale scrunching gravel and trod gently on the velvety border of grass that edged the drive. They stole round the house like thieves, and found their way up to Mollie's bedroom. That young lady hopped round on one foot waving her flags triumphantly.

"I guessed it ages ago," she said, forgetting in her excitement that "ages ago" was only yesterday morning - it was really very difficult to keep pace with a Time that behaved so erratically - "Something Aunt Mary told me about having a green diamond made me wonder. That's why I knew him before you did. Now Hugh will be our uncle. My goodness!"

The tale of the Desmond O'Rourke conversation convinced even the unwilling Dick that Major

Campbell was Hugh the inventor, but he still refused to share Mollie's conviction that there was a romance connecting him with Aunt Mary. "You girls are so jolly sentimental," he said impatiently. "Why *should* Aunt Mary want to go and get engaged to a chap old enough to be her father, or at any rate her uncle, just as I have arrived. I bet I play a better game of golf than he does, and even Bemister says my tennis has improved a lot this term."

"*I* agree with Mollie," said Jerry, trying to look romantic, "I thought so first go-off, as soon as he said 'Miss Gordon'; there's a look -"

"If it's the look you think you've got on just now it's a fairly imbecile one," Dick interrupted scornfully. "Perhaps you are in love with Mollie!"

Mollie, who was rather tired, was leaning back against her pillows, her bandaged foot lying on the bed and the other foot swinging over the side. Her short, blue-serge skirt was at its shortest and made no pretence at hiding her serviceable blue knickers, from which emerged a pair of useful girl-guidish legs, suitably clad in black merino stockings and lace-up shoes. Her bobbed hair was for the moment rough and tumbled, and she still held her flags spread out on either side of her. No one could have looked less romantic, and they all three had to laugh at Dick's suggestion. He cheered up slightly.

"Anyhow - now perhaps we can find out a few things - what the blood was, and how rich the diamond-mine made them."

"And if Grizzel made her fortune in jam," Mollie added, "and if Hugh ever invented an aeroplane."

"He's in the R.A.F.," Jerry remarked, "we saw it on the card he gave us."

This reminder cheered Dick up still more. If his favourite aunt had the bad taste to throw over a promising football nephew for anything so wishy-washy as a lover, it was consoling to know that the wisher-washer might include an aeroplane. "Perhaps he'll take us up one of these days if we behave nicely about Aunt Polly-wolly-doodle," he said hopefully; "that is, if there really is anything in Mollie's tosh. He looks an aged old party to be turning somersaults in the air, I must say."

The welcome sound of the tea-bell put an end to their discussion, and soon Dick was drowning his sorrows in strawberries and cream. It was rather a bad - or good - sign that Aunt Mary and the mysterious Major Campbell were absent, but on the whole it was a relief. Only a somewhat preoccupied Grannie was there to attend to their wants. No one spoke very much. There was a slightly depressing atmosphere about that tea, so carefully prepared by the missing aunt. The place where she usually sat looked extraordinarily empty, much emptier, Mollie thought, than it did when her aunt merely happened to be out. As soon as tea was over the boys went off to visit the puppies again; Grannie, still inclined to be silent and absent-minded, sat down to her knitting; and Mollie, feeling somehow more lonely than she had done before the boys came, wandered into the deserted morning-room. She picked up a book she had been interested in yesterday, but it had lost its flavour and she soon laid it down and went over to the window, where she stood looking out at the wet garden. It was raining in earnest now, not heavily but steadily; little pools were collecting in the gravel, rose-petals were dropping in showers, and the flowers in the herbaceous borders were beginning to look as if they had had enough rain for the present and would welcome now a chance to dry themselves. Mollie opened the window wide and seated herself sideways on the sill, heedless of the raindrops that blew against her face and blouse. For a long time she stared out into the rain, seeing not the well-kept garden before her, but the cypress-bordered path in that other garden.

The sound of the clock striking made her turn her head and look indoors. The room looked dark and dull. Aunt Mary's work-basket stood open on the table, with her work lying where she had flung it down when she ran out to meet Mollie. The jig-saw puzzle was tidied away, and the sofa cushions sat in a prim row on the sofa, with nothing about them to show how often a kind hand had tucked them in behind a young invalid's back. The volume of Shakespeare still lay on a side-table, and reminded Mollie freshly of Prue's first visit.

"I am being sorry for myself," she thought, "and of all the useless things - ! I will go upstairs and change my frock and tidy my hair, and then write to Mother. And when the boys come in we must find something to do. It is simply horrid of me to be moping round because dear Aunt Mary is happy, especially as it is the very thing I was keen on yesterday. I feel as if I lived in the middle of one of Hugh's shadow-clocks," she sighed as she went slowly upstairs, "with Yesterday and To-morrow going round me all the time, and my own shadow falling on them both." This poetic fancy rather pleased her, and she decided to put on her best evening frock and fasten her hair with a rose velvet bandeau.

She was clasping a pale coral necklace round her throat

　　　　Lydia Miller Middleton

when there came a tap at the door, followed by "May I come in?" and then Aunt Mary herself appeared. And such a radiant and smiling Aunt Mary that all Mollie's depression vanished in the twinkling of an eye. She hurried across the room and gave Mollie a hug.

"Why - how pretty you have made yourself, Mollie darling. That is sweet of you, for I want you to look your very best this evening. I have a most astonishing piece of news for you - why do you laugh, you naughty girl? I don't see how you can possibly have guessed, and I am sure Grannie didn't tell you."

Mollie laughed again as she returned her aunt's hug: "It was not so frightfully difficult to guess, after what you said about the green diamond ring yesterday - why, you have got it on! It *is* lovely, isn't it? I think it is *just* as beautiful -" Mollie stopped in some confusion, "I mean it is the loveliest ring I ever saw. If I ever get engaged I should like one exactly the same."

"I hope it will bring you a little more luck than it brought us to begin with," Aunt Mary said, with a sigh, looking down at the hand which lay in Mollie's. "It is ten years since I got it, and if you had asked me yesterday I should have said it would perhaps be another ten before I could wear it like this, but all sorts of wonderful things happened all of a sudden and here we are! But I cannot understand why you guessed anything yesterday, you funny child. I am sure I said very little."

"It wasn't what you *said*, it was how you *looked*. And you didn't hear yourself sighing, Aunt Polly-wolly-doodle. We were doing *As You Like It* at school before I got measles, and we learnt something about people in love, I can tell you!" Mollie nodded her head wisely. "I am not romantic myself like the girl who was doing Rosalind, but I'm not *quite* so blind as a bat is, and I came up with Major Campbell this afternoon."

"Dear me!" Aunt Mary exclaimed with a laugh, "you are getting dreadfully grown-up, Mollie. I hope you don't - that you don't think my dear old Hugh is really old, because he happens to have rather white hair. It is the heart that counts, and his blessed old heart is as young as yours. Now I must run and dress. Call the boys and tell them to come in and be nice to their new uncle. You have simply *got* to be friends."

Half an hour later three exceedingly tidy and rather prim young people were formally introduced to "Uncle Hugh", who surveyed them gravely through a pair of gold-rimmed eyeglasses. Mollie was not sure whether a twinkle she thought she saw belonged to the eyes or to the glasses. "I could almost believe that he remembers the Time-travellers," she said to herself. But if he did he gave no further sign of it, nor could the children see much trace of the boy Hugh in this keen-eyed, white-haired, brown-skinned stranger.

"I suppose you are detesting me with all your might," he remarked as they seated themselves. "You have all my sympathy. I should detest myself if I were you. But you have had her for a good many years, haven't you? It is high time that she flew off with me."

"Is she going to fly?" Dick asked with interest. "I could put up with getting married myself if my wife came in an aeroplane and took me for a jolly good flight. I could chuck her out if I didn't like her," he added, with a grin.

"The very first time I ever flew in my life," Major Campbell said, "was in a balloon, and I played at the game of chucking out, and got a fright which I am convinced caused my hair to turn prematurely grey. Would you like to hear about it?"

"Ra-*ther*!" Dick and Jerry replied together. (Now perhaps the mystery of the blood might be explained.)

So Major Campbell told them the story that they already knew nearly as well as he did himself - in fact, Mollie found herself on the point of correcting him upon one or two points. He told it well, better than he had done on that agitating occasion so many years ago, but - he did not divulge the mystery.

It was almost too tantalizing to be endured. Mollie had to keep repeating to herself "A Guide's Word is *Always* to be Trusted," as she reflected upon that most provoking promise extracted from her by Prue. It was so long ago, surely a question, one question, would not matter now. Unfortunately it was also, as Mollie expressed it to herself "so short ago" that she could remember Prue's words only too plainly: "*You must not ask questions however much you want to.*" It is true that she had broken the rule once, but it had been in forgetfulness, not deliberately. Dick and Jerry were perhaps less picturesque in the manner of their vows, but they certainly had no intention of breaking them. It was Aunt Mary who unconsciously came to the rescue:

"And what *was* the blood that wasn't blood?"

"Oh, that! That was merely - that was merely -" Major Campbell stopped and began to laugh.

"Merely what? Be quick," said dear Aunt Mary, "we are longing to know."

"I am sorry - I hate to let you down, but it was only dye. Desmond had a notion that he could make a fortune with a native dye factory - vegetable dyes, you know. But it never came to anything. I think it is rather a pity he didn't persevere; he might have done something with it."

Dye! Well, of all the prosaic endings to a thrilling tale! And yet, when the children came to think of it, what else could it have been? They were annoyed at themselves for not thinking of such an obvious thing. Major Campbell laughed again when he saw the blank look on three faces.

"It's a poor end-up, isn't it?" he said. "Why did you force me into it? But there is still the stone, if you would like to see it. You will find it over there on the writing-table."

Dick fetched the stone - the identical stone they had last seen in Hugh's hand forty years ago. After all, the end was not so prosaic!

It looked little the worse for its adventures through Time and Space as it lay in Dick's hand. An inscription had been scratched in and inked over:

Hugh Campbell }
    August 4th, 1880.
Desmond O'Rourke }
Mary Gordon. 1910.

They looked at in silence for a minute.

"It reminds me of a tombstone," Dick remarked cheerfully, "if you wrote 'Wife of the Aboves' under Aunt Mary's name it would look jolly mysterious."

"Grand-daughter of one of the aboves would be more appropriate," Major Campbell said ruefully, smoothing the back of his grey head with one hand, while with the other he gave a gentle tug to a stray lock of Aunt Mary's pretty brown hair.

"Fiddlesticks!" Aunt Mary said briskly. "We'll get you a wig if you feel so badly about it, or perhaps Desmond would dye you a nice bright red. No - I'll tell you what would be really interesting - if you could write on your stone the names of all the people whose lives it dropped into that day. There are Desmond and Prue and their children" (Jerry looked up with a startled glance), "and their wonderful grandchild" (Jerry's eyes were round with dismay. Farewell, Romance!), "and Grizzel and Jack and *their* children, for Grizzel would never have met Jack if Prue hadn't married Desmond. And there's me, for if you hadn't got tangled up with the O'Rourkes we should probably never have met, even though our greats and grands were such friends. Then we may add Dick's name to our list, for I mean to have him out in Australia one of these days, and perhaps Jerry too - who knows! And Mollie may go green-diamond hunting among the young O'Rourkes - Brian would do nicely." Aunt Mary laughed mischievously at Mollie.

"That *would* be a sermon in stones and no mistake," Major Cambell said, with a smile. "We should require a regular palimpsest to hold them all. Think of Grizzel and all the pies she loves to have her fingers in - all those people on their fruit farm for instance, mostly people who have been down on their luck one way or another. And the young persons she has helped with what she calls their artistic careers. And Prue with her army of Girl Guides!"

"And all through one little stone," Aunt Mary said, taking the stone into her own hand and looking at it thoughtfully.

"I expect the green diamond had more to do with it than the stone, really," Mollie said dreamily, thinking to herself that if Desmond had not found the ring he would not have troubled to seek for the stone-thrower. She would have pursued this interesting line of thought had not someone at that moment trod upon her well foot, and someone else pinched an arm hard. These delicate attentions brought her back to reality and she felt that she had "dropped a brick" pretty badly. Aunt Mary looked puzzled, and Major Campbell's eyes twinkled - or was it his eye-glasses?

"The diamond may have been a temptation," he said, "but I hope it wasn't such a bribe as all that comes to. You have to remember that she might have stuck to the ring and thrown me over any time all these years."

Mollie breathed a sigh of relief. Her words had evidently been misunderstood - or had he understood and come to her help? She wished he would take off those glasses!

"Catch her!" Dick was saying indignantly, "Aunt Mary is a jolly good old sport! You don't know her half as well as I do if *that* is what you think."

"Don't I?" said Major Campbell, turning to look at

Aunt Mary, who was beginning to show signs of embarrassment under so much scrutiny. He took off his eye-glasses, but immediately replaced them by a pair of large round tortoise-shell spectacles through which he gazed at her solemnly.

"What *are* you doing, Hugh? Take off those absurd things this moment," Aunt Mary commanded as the children laughed.

"I am looking at you through stronger glasses," he answered. "I thought perhaps I wasn't seeing you properly, but the better I see the prettier you look."

"My hat!" Dick exclaimed, "look at Aunt Mary blushing. She's the colour of a ripe red currant. I think it's time we did a bunk. Come on, you kids!"

Late that evening Mollie sat at the open window again, this time to watch for the boys, who had set out for a belated round of golf. The rain had ceased and the air was fresh and sweet, but the lingering twilight was darkened by clouds and the garden was veiled in a ghostly white mist. Mollie had been listening to talk of times old and new, and now Grannie had settled down to her nightly game of patience, Major Campbell was seated in a deep and roomy arm-chair, and Aunt Mary had gone to the piano.

"Play the old tunes you played me to sleep with," Mollie begged. "I think I like old tunes best of all."

" So do I , Mollie," said Major Campbell. "Do you remember Prue's old musical-box, Mary? It is still in existence. Prue always turns it out on the dear old pater's birthday and has a sort of memorial service -

I'm glad he didn't live to see the war. He was such a softhearted, confiding old chap, and never could be induced to see the black spots in poor human nature - he was always ready with an excuse for any lapse from virtue. He never could screw himself up to the pitch of giving his children a thorough good rowing, though I am sure we often needed one badly enough."

Aunt Mary's fingers wandered vaguely over the piano for a few minutes, and then she began to sing:

"Oft in the stilly night
Ere slumber's chain hath bound me,
Fond memory brings the light
Of other days around me."

It seemed to Mollie that she could hear the silvery tinkle of Prue's musical-box again, and see Papa's kind blue eyes.

As she listened to the music and gazed into the misty garden, she saw, as she thought, the boys standing in the shadow of the black Cedar of Lebanon across the way. She leaned forward, wondering why they lingered there so silently. It was not easy to see in the on-coming darkness - surely there were *three* figures, and two of them looked like girls. Her heart gave a sudden jump - yes, she could plainly make out two girls and a boy. She slipped through the window and crossed the terraced drive.

* * * * *

There they were - dear Prue, with Grizzel clinging to one arm, and Hugh in the background - oh, how Mollie longed to keep them!

"I was thinking of you, Prue," she said eagerly, "I wanted you so much. If you could only stay!"

Prue shook her head, with a smile. "No, we have only come to say good-bye, Mollie. Your Time-travelling is over for this time, you won't come to our Time any more. Did you like it?"

"I *loved* it," Mollie answered fervently, not pausing to ask herself whether it was the Time or the children that she had loved. "If only it could be *now*, Prue, so that you could stay!"

But Prue shook her head again: "We've got to go. Perhaps some day we will meet again - Time-travellers often do. I think that's why - that's why - " she knit her pretty brows in the effort to express a difficult thought.

"Hush!" Grizzel said suddenly, "she is singing 'I shot an arrow into the air'; Mamma sings that and I love it. I want to listen; may we go nearer?"

They tip-toed across the gravel, and stood in the shadow of the lamp-lit window.

"I breathed a song into the air,
It fell to earth I know not where,
For who has sight so swift and strong
That it can follow the flight of a song?

"Long, long afterwards, in an oak
I found the arrow still unbroke.
And the song from beginning to end
I found again, in the heart of a friend."

"I love that," Grizzel whispered. "Papa says you often do find the song long, long afterwards. I think it's something like casting your bread upon the waters, though I never could understand why they chose *bread*. I shouldn't think there would be much of it left after many days in the water. I like a song better."

Hugh had stepped nearer to the window, and was observing the interior of the room with curious eyes. "Who's the old buffer with white hair?" he asked.

Mollie began to laugh, but suddenly stopped. She looked from the boy to the man - so there *were* two Hughs! "He is a Time-traveller," she answered softly, "but he has travelled the other way, forwards, you know. He has invented a lot of things about flying."

"Has he!" exclaimed Hugh. "That old chap!" He leaned forward and gazed more intently at the white-haired man. "I wish I was him," he said wistfully!

"Cooo-eee!"

The call seemed to come from far away, muffled, perhaps, by the night air.

"They are calling us," said Prue. "We must go - come, Hugh. Good-bye, Mollie, goodbye."

* * * * *

" Where are you, Mollie, my child?" Aunt Mary had risen and was coming towards the window. Mollie turned to answer her.

"All right, Aunt Mary. I am here looking for the boys."

"Are the boys not there? I thought I heard voices." Aunt Mary leaned out and peered into the dark. "How dark it is - I can't see - I thought for a moment I saw someone there - here they are coming!"

"Cooo-eee! Where are you, Moll? We want you."

"It's Dick calling," Mollie said. "I'll go and meet them, Aunt Mary; it's only a step. Coming, Dick," she called back.

But she found it hard to walk on the wet gravel without her stick, and after sending another call to the boys stood and waited where she was, wondering why she had not felt her foot when she had gone to the other children. She stared into the shadows of the cedar, but the little figures had disappeared. "I love them," she murmured to herself, "and I can never forget this week, whether I ever learn to understand Time-travelling or not. I mean to learn ever so much about Australia and our other colonies, and about the immigrant ships Prue talked of. I am glad she is a Guider and that I am a Guide." She looked back to the lighted window, through which she could see Aunt Mary and Major Campbell standing together, then forward into the misty dark - she could hear the boys coming up the hill. "I loved Prue and Grizzel and their Time," she repeated, "and of course Aunt Mary is going to have a tremendously happy time now, but - I am glad that *I* belong to Dick and Jerry. I like our own Time best; it suits us. It's a good sort of Time for doing things, and it will be better before we are done with it, if we all Carry On.

"I'm here, Dick!"